THE COWGIRL'S FAKE BILLIONAIRE MARRIAGE

BILLIONAIRE HEARTS RANCH SERIES BOOK FOUR

EDITH MACKENZIE

Even when you feel like you are lost, remember there is a plan for everything. Have faith

PROLOGUE

Above a sea of rooftops, the mountain range rose majestically skywards, towering over the mere mortals below. Chora sat on the back step of her grandmother's house, dejectedly staring out at the foreign vista. For all of her eight years, she'd been happy as a clam in Texas with her horse, Prince, and her best friend, Misty. Why did Dad have to go and lose his stupid job? It wasn't fair that they'd made her leave. *Misty probably already had a new best friend. Probably that annoying Indie or that girl who was always drawing —what was her name? Evelyn?* At least Dad and Mom got to see stuff. She'd just waved them off as they went in search of work. Back home she'd be going for a ride on Prince. Chora sniffled. She'd made sure that the girl who'd bought him had known that he loved bananas and not carrots and that he liked to have a spot near his ear scratched. He'd probably already forgotten her, too.

"What you up to, peanut?" Grandma eased herself gingerly down onto the step beside her.

"Nothing." Chora wiped at her face to erase any evidence

otherwise with all the dignity an eight-year-old could manage.

"Hmm." The old woman stared out into the distance. "Something I've learned over the years is that life goes on whether you like it or not. You can only control what's in front of you right now, not what's behind you in the rearview mirror. Look at your dad and mom. Do you think they want to be living back here at home with me? Not that I don't love having you here, but I'm sure your mom is missing having her own home. But they're out there putting their best face on and trying to move forward." Grandma wrapped an arm around Chora's skinny shoulders. "Now, wash your face and get a drink of water. We have somewhere we need to be."

"Where?" Chora scratched at a scab on her knee from one of the last things she'd done in Texas.

"Go and do what I said, and you'll find out."

Abuzz with curiosity, Chora moved faster than she had in days and before long she was clicking her seatbelt into place. "I don't mean to be all..."

"Sulky?" Grandma answered for her, checking for traffic.

"I was going to say glum. I just miss everything back home." She swallowed over the ever-present tightness in her throat.

"I know, honey, but there's a lot to appreciate here, too. For example, Texas has three types of venomous snakes. In California, we only have *The Real Housewives of OC*."

Chora giggled, only half understanding the reference since her mother insisted she was still too young to watch the show. "What else?"

"Um, in Texas they ride bulls, and here they ride waves, and we have mountains and hills. We might even go up and see some snow soon."

"What about flowers? Bluebonnets were my favorite. I

couldn't wait till they bloomed each year." Chora was starting to feel a little better.

"We have something even more special, because it doesn't happen each year. But when the conditions are right, say once every ten or so years, we get a desert wildflower bloom in Death Valley. Plus, the weather's nicer here." Grandma winked at her before pulling into a park. "We're here."

The building Chora found herself staring at was gray and cold looking. Slipping her hands into the pockets of her shorts, she trailed behind her grandmother, not entirely looking forward to finding out where they were going anymore. They passed through some glass doors and a linoleum lined room and then another door, and Chora found herself standing in between rows of cages.

She slowly made her way down them, hopeless eyes following her movements, until she dropped to her knees, overwhelmed and clutching at the mesh. All these animals—abused, unwanted and abandoned. Stomach twisting in knots, Chora drew in a deep breath. A wet tongue on her fingers startled her into looking up. A scrawny, brindle puppy was gazing at her with huge, adoring, hopeful eyes. Gently, she reached through to pet his head, his entire body overtaken with wiggling happiness.

"I think you've made a friend there," Grandma said behind her. "Would you like to take him out and hold him?"

A fluttery sensation replaced the knots in her belly. "You mean I can?"

Grandma laughed. "It's an animal shelter, of course you can. In fact, that's what these poor beasts need the most—love. Whenever I volunteer here, I always end up staying hours longer than I mean to because I need to make sure all the animals get some loving."

Chora's foot twitched as she watched the gate being opened, and then the puppy bounded straight into her waiting arms. "Poor little darlin'. What did they do to you?" In answer, he licked her face, seemingly not content until he'd covered every square inch.

"He was found abandoned in a plastic bag with his litter mates. He was the only one that survived."

Rage singed away the self-pity she'd been indulging in since she'd been made to move to California. "How can anyone do that?"

"I don't know, but they do. More than I'd like to admit." Grandma smiled fondly at her. "I haven't had a dog at the house since old Jasper died. Maybe it's time we got another one."

The puppy wiggled in Chora's arms. She could feel the bones swimming in a fur coat that felt too big for it. "Do you really mean that?"

"Yeah."

"What about the others?" Chora struggled to breathe at the thought of all the despairing eyes that would be left behind.

"We can't help them. At least, not today." Grandma's shoulders stooped, infinite sadness on her face. "No matter how much we might want to."

Chora cuddled her puppy close. She might not be able to save them all today, but she vowed with all of her young heart that, one day, she would.

CHAPTER 1

"You spell it C-H-O-R-A" she said to the barista for the millionth time. Today was not the day to keep her waiting for her first coffee hit of the morning. "Look, all I want is a latte and some of that chocolate cake, I don't really care what name you put on it."

Finding a spare table, Chora sat down and pulled her phone from her pocket to once again look at the dog's photo. She couldn't understand why anyone would be so cruel. But while there were people out there who treated animals despicably, her charity would be there to pick up the pieces and make sure all the critters were safe and loved. Chora glanced at her watch. Maybe she should have ordered the cake to go. She had to get to the hotel to make sure everything was going to plan for tonight's gala fundraising fashion show. It had been insane since the famous model, Shelby Erikson, had agreed to a favor for her sister-in-law. The phone had been ringing off the hook with people trying to get a ticket to what had become the hottest show in town. Misty, her long-time friend and patron, had assured her that, with what they would raise tonight, the Animals Are Forever charity wouldn't have to worry about money for a long time.

"Coral? Soy decaf latte for Coral?" called the barista, gesturing at Chora when she wasn't quick to approach the counter.

Chora pushed her hair impatiently from her face as she stood, stowing the phone away. *For Pete's sake, the dude had one job to do...*

She was still fuming about not getting the caffeine fix she'd been craving as she made her way across town to check in on the fashion show prep. Chora knew Misty would be in her element arranging it, but it was the Animals Are Forever charity name on the line and she felt personally responsible. The fact was, she always did. All the animals that she was yet to help were counting on her to get everything perfect.

When she was a little girl and still living in Texas, her dad had been a stickler for, if you say you're going to do a job, sticking with it till the job was done. Back then it had been going out to feed the animals on the ranch, no matter the weather conditions, but now it was her mantra in life. *100% the cowgirl way or hit the highway!*

Making her way into the venue, she was greeted with a controlled chaos. She got the sense that it was only through the tight vigilance of those in charge that stopped it descending into a ruckus.

"This show is going to blow people's minds when they see it." Misty materialized at her side.

Chora nodded, eyes still scanning the sea of humanity that seemed to be swirling around on currents she couldn't quite fathom. "You've outdone yourself this year."

"I'd love to take all the credit, but I really can't." Misty gave a humble shrug. "When I mentioned it to Mr Onissios that he might allow us to use some of his capsule pieces, he went one further and not only gave permission for that, but also designed some just for this show that we can auction. Then Evelyn decided she wanted a break from big art installations and came out with the jewelry and headpieces. Throw in Shelby declaring she had to walk the show, and then Ash Cooper, the famous actress, found out about it from her makeup artist and simply would not take no for an answer. It snowballed without any help from me." A gleam appeared in her eyes as she gave Chora a sideways glance. "Actually, I can take outright credit for one thing, and to be fair, it's the real icing on the cake. Getting Presley Barnett to come and perform with her mother for the first time since the birth of her daughter—that moved a whole heap of tickets."

"I was amazed when you said you'd gotten her to agree to come." Chora had been a fan of the country singer for years.

"It's amazing who you meet in Las Vegas. Now that I'm finished patting myself on the back, do you want to have a final run-through of which animals are getting paired to which outfit and model? Shelby's already laid claim to the pot-bellied pig, and Ash wants to walk the alpaca. I actually think that, out of all the girls here, they probably have the best chance of controlling them."

Chora chuckled at the possible mayhem that could break out on the catwalk. "Well, they are the only cowgirls in the crew. I think it's a great choice. Speaking of which, I believe congratulations are in order." She gave Shelby a hug as she joined them.

The model flashed her trademark broad grin. "Thanks. I'm still getting used to the idea that I'm hitched. And does this mean I get the pig?"

"Do you want to see some photos?" Misty pulled her phone out. "As sister-in-law to the bride and best friend of the groom, I made sure I got plenty." She winked at the blushing bride.

Chora nodded and flicked through the images. They were

filled with a laughing Shelby and her husband and family. "Did you have it on William's island?"

"Neither of us could think of a place we wanted it to happen more, and obviously we could keep it super private with just our nearest and dearest. Then we followed it with a honeymoon starting there with just our families and then on to Paris and Myanmar. It was perfect." Judging from her glowing expression, married life was definitely treating her well.

Envy skittered through Chora. *I wonder what it's like to be in love like that.* Her last relationship had ended several years ago due to her commitment to her charity and there'd been no one since. *I'd have to date to even have a chance, and that ain't happening anytime soon.*

"Tell her what you got William for a wedding present." Misty nudged her sister-in-law.

Shelby rolled her eyes as she laughed. "It's not that big of a deal."

Misty raised her brows sky high. "Oh, but it is. Now tell her."

The model satisfied herself with another eyeroll before complying. "I got him some chickens."

Chora had only met with Misty's business partner a few times, but never figured him for a chicken man—and she was normally pretty good at matching animals to people. "Oh."

"That's what I said." Misty nudged Shelby, chuckling.

The model put her hands on her hips. "Well, he loves Nugget and Drumstick."

Chora snorted. "I'm not really sure he does if he named them that."

"He said it was to motivate them into being good egg layers, and he's very clever at those sorts of things." Shelby glared defiantly at each of them, challenging them to disagree.

Chora threw her hands up in the air in defeat. "Who am I to say that isn't the case?" She rubbed her hands together. "It's only a few hours before showtime. Misty, what do you need me to do?"

"Oh, so much. Come with me." Chora followed her friend. *Please let this be a success,* she prayed. *The animals really need it.*

~

"HOW MUCH?" screeched Chora, aware that her voice was alarmingly high-pitched. It was a wonder that no dogs were howling in protest.

"Three million, four hundred and fifty-two thousand and fifty dollars." Misty looked up from her spreadsheet. "I did round it down to that fifty dollars, I hope you don't mind."

"Mind? This is—" Chora clutched at her chest. "I mean, we've done some amazing fundraisers, but this is … I think I need to sit down." She collapsed onto a chair, trying to make sense of it all, a wonderful sense of relief washing over her. No animal would have to be turned away. Burying her face in her hands, she began to cry.

"Hey, we're meant to be happy. This is good news." Misty put an arm around her sobbing friend. "We did it. The Animals Are Forever charity will be well funded for the next few years. Obviously, I will continue to host fundraising events because the animals never can have too much money in their corner, but this means you won't have to count every penny."

We can help every animal that needs it. "I can't thank you enough." Chora said, finally calming herself down.

"You're the one who does all the hard work. I just swan in and take the credit for parting some of my rich friends from their spare change." Misty looked her in the eye. "What you do, Chora, it's special and it needs to be done."

"And now that you've made the charity financially secure, I can." Chora sat, taking it all in, the situation making her curiously numb now that the initial shock had retreated. "And it's going to make a difference. You wait and see."

LANDON NODDED at one of the old boys who had just entered the club before returning his attention to his friends. "Anyway, the crux of it all is that it has to happen before I turn thirty."

His friend, Stirling, shifted uncomfortably in his chair, staring into his glass of port like it held the answers to the universe within. Freddy, for his part, simply gaped at Landon in horrified stupor. "But that's only two months away," he protested.

It was only Alistair who focused keen eyes on Landon. "What the bloody heck are you going to do?" *You could take the Aussie and educate him in Eton and Cambridge, but he still remained firmly an Aussie in times of stress,* Landon mused.

"I'll figure something out. There's no way I'm going to let my uncle profit from all of this. He'll just blow it all. I need it for my research and to continue funding the dig in Crete."

"What do you need from us, old chap?" Stirling finally joined the conversation.

"Help with where to start." Turmoil still rolled through Landon, but he felt slightly better now that his friends were onside. Really, how hard could this be?

CHAPTER 2

The horse stood swaying on its feet, exhausted from its escape into freedom. A back once strong now swayed under the weight of age, the horse's eyes dulled of all joy. Chora's heart broke for what the old mare had endured. "It's gonna be okay, honey," she crooned, her voice thick with unshed tears. "You're safe now."

"Chora, if you can make sure she stays still, I'll start examining her," the vet instructed, getting his stethoscope out. "Although, I don't see much life in this poor old girl."

She stroked the rough, patchy hide, the hair brittle under her hand. "Darlin', he's just going to give you a once-over, and then we can start working out how to make you feel better."

The vet moved about his work, gentle movements belying the dryness of his voice. "This one might be too far gone."

"How sick is she?"

"She's old, Chora."

"So? She still deserves a chance," she fired back at him. The mare didn't even twitch at the vehement denial. *Not a good sign.*

"You're going to sink a lot of money into a horse that might only live for another year. Wouldn't that money be better spent on younger animals?"

"She might live a year, or she might live longer. But whatever time she does have, I'm going to make sure it's spent being loved and cared for. Don't worry about the money." There was something about the old horse that reminded her of the one she'd been forced to leave behind in her childhood. She'd hate to think this is how he ended up. Luckily, she knew he'd died peacefully of old age, cherished till the end and buried under his favorite tree.

The vet gave her a searching glance. "You're the boss." He rummaged for his thermometer. "Easy, old girl, I'm just going to take your temperature." Chora continued to stroke the mare, but she wasn't sure if she even knew she was there. "Okay, Chora, here's where it's at. She's malnourished, needs a course of worming and probably has Cushing's. It's going to be a fine balancing act to get the weight back on her and not have any flareups." He stopped speaking and shook his head ruefully. "And I should just stop speaking because nothing I say is going to stop you from returning her to full health." He handed her a bottle. "Give her this course of antibiotics and worm her. I'll come back in a week to check on her." The vet paused briefly before picking up his toolbox. "You know, I think you're doing great things here, but sometimes you need to make the hard decision on who to save."

"And I do—more than I'd like to—but this mare can be saved, and that's what we're going to do." Chora smiled despite her chin lifting defiantly. Sensing that there was nothing more she would welcome from him, the vet left.

Chora rummaged in her pocket and fished her phone out, dialing it. "Hi, Wyatt," she greeted when the owner of Hope Springs Horse Rescue answered.

"Hey, Chora, what have you got for me?"

"Who says I have anything?"

"Because you only call me when you have another guest you'd like to send my way."

Chora smiled at his droll words. He kind of had her there. "Okay, you got me. I have a lovely old gal that will need somewhere to spend the rest of her days. That is, once she's in a stable enough condition to handle the trip."

"Sure thing, Chora. You know we take all comers. How bad is she?"

"Old and neglected, but nothing I can't fix." Chora wished she felt as confident as she sounded.

"I'll let Kelly know to expect another one." She could almost hear his smile through the phone when he mentioned his girlfriend.

"How's Kelly?"

"Oh, you know, running around trying to keep me in line. But I've figured out a way to keep her busy for the next little while."

"Oh? Do tell."

"Yeah, I've got her organizing our wedding."

"What?" Chora exploded. "Is this your way of telling me you're finally going to make an honest woman out of Kelly? About time!"

Wyatt laughed through the phone. "I'm gonna try, and that's almost exactly what Quinn said, too. Are you sure you're not Australian?"

"Not that I'm aware of, but I'm sure Great-Granny had more than a few wartime skeletons in her closet. You know I expect an invitation, right?"

"Expect one before the year is out. I need to get back to it. I've got an orphaned foal here that needs to be fed. Just let me know when the mare's good to travel, and I'll arrange transport for her."

There really were good people out there, and Wyatt and

his soon-to-be wife were some of the best. Chora always felt better when she talked to one of her friends, and she couldn't help but smile as she hung up.

"So, like, there's this thing I'm trying, you know, since it's super hard to meet a man here—or at least one with money." Chora frowned, confused at the sudden intrusion into her thoughts. Blinking, she looked to find the owner of the nasally voice. *Ahh, Christina.*

"I don't really know too much about the dating scene here," Chora admitted to the peroxide blonde woman. Looks could be deceiving, and at face value, Christina had more in common with Malibu Barbie than someone who would volunteer at an animal rescue charity. Over the last year, Christina had proved herself to be trustworthy and committed.

"Well, take my word for it, it's HARD." Christina fiddled with the pendant at her neck with her long, pink taloned nails, the little diamantes catching the light. "So, I've taken the necessary steps to up my game."

Chora frowned, not sure where this conversation was going to end. "Which is?"

"I've signed up with a Billionaire Matchmaker." Christina said, finishing with an excited squeal as she clapped her hands.

"Why?" *Since when was that even a thing?*

"Weren't you listening? Because it's hard to find some-one." Christina looked at her like she was dense.

"No, I got the meeting people is hard part of it, but why a Billionaire Matchmaker?" *Did billionaire's even need to use one? Surely they had women lining up around the block.*

"Because, like, why wouldn't you want to marry a billion-aire? The shopping, the houses in exotic locations, not work-ing, the clothes." With each item added to her list, Christina's eyes grew wider at her imagined riches. Chora couldn't think of a lifestyle she would want less. It all sounded so materialistic and vain. "Anyway," Christina ploughed on. "I have my first date tomorrow night and he's gorgeous! And did I mention he's disgustingly rich?"

"Um, good luck." Chora tried to muster some enthusiasm to put into her words, but all she really wanted was to end the conversation so she could go home to her animals.

"I really think he's The One." Christina fell into step beside her. "I'll make sure to tell you all about it." *Yay.* "Every juicy detail."

Chora was still mulling over Christina's determination to marry a billionaire as she fed her animals that night. There were Mr Hoppikins and Mrs Cottontail—the bunnies—the old ginger tom cat called Tom who only had one eye, the tabby cat missing the end of its tail called Spot and, of course, Mac-attack, the macaw that had come to her completely bald. She knew a few billionaires and they all had great lives, but she wouldn't trade hers for all the money in the world.

"Ahchoo!" Chora winced as she watched the sneezing Christina make her way down the corridor to her. "Ahchoo, ahchoo, ahchoo." She stopped to blow her nose. "I'm sick."

"I can see that. You need to go home and go to bed. Sleep's the best medicine." Chora took a step back from the blotchy-faced woman, her nose an alarming shade of scarlet. "I don't know why you didn't just stay there this morning and call in sick."

"Because I have my billionaire date tonight," snuffled Christina.

Honestly, I have to give the girl credit for tenacity. "Well, cancel."

"I can't," wailed the blonde woman. "It's one of the conditions of the matchmaker accepting you. Once you agree to a date, you have to go through with it. If I cancel, she won't match me up with anyone else, unless—" Her bloodshot eyes fastened on Chora. "You could go in my place."

"That will never work." Chora backed up so rapidly she hit the wall behind her.

"We're both blondes, and it's not like he's ever seen me in real life. He won't notice the difference." Dubiously, Chora looked from her natural honey blonde hair to Christina's peroxide locks. She should probably feel offended. "All you need to do is go on the date with him and pretend to be me and—ahchoo—then I just won't go on another one with him. I'll say there wasn't any chemistry—ahchoo—and then she'll have to match me with another billionaire when I'm feeling better." Chora was shocked at how coldly calculating the other woman was about finding love. *Were there even that many bachelor billionaires around?*

"I don't really think it's a good idea." Chora shifted her weight, trying to gauge her best escape path.

"I'll do poo patrol for a month," pleaded Christina. "All you have to do is have a nice dinner with a rich man, no strings attached. And did I mention I'll owe you? Please," wheedled the desperate woman. "It's taken me months to get approved for this matchmaker, and now it's all going to be ruined because I got sick." Christina deployed her best puppy dog eyes, only slightly ruined by their weepiness.

"Fine, but it's poo patrol for two months and you need to bring me a coffee and donut every morning."

"Deal."

"Now go home. I don't want you getting me or any of the volunteers sick." What had she just gotten herself into?

CHAPTER 3

What exactly did one wear on a date with a billionaire? If he was a Texan billionaire like her friend's husband, Colt, anything Chora owned would be suitable. But if he was more like Misty's fashion-loving business partner, William, then she was in serious trouble. Why had she agreed to this?

Defeated, she gathered Mr Hoppikins from the floor and cuddled him on her lap, resisting the urge to pick up the phone and tell Christina she'd changed her mind. Who was she kidding? She wasn't the type to let someone down when she'd given her word. Rubbing the rabbit's velveteen ears gently between her fingers, she ran through some possible outfit options in her mind. *Maybe the serape print dress with a pair of heels?* Chora giggled. At least he wouldn't miss her in the bright colors. Spying Mac-attack on her dresser helping himself to her jewelry box, she carefully deposited the bunny on her bed before leaping to her feet and saving a beaded earring from the macaw.

"Dude, how many times have I told you? Not for you," she

admonished the non-repentant bird who stared back at her with assumed innocence as he strutted onto her hand.

"Good boy, Mac-attack. Best birdie in world." The parrot bopped as he made his pronouncement.

"Really, Mac-attack? You think now's the time to throw those words at me?" Chora strove to arrange her features into stern lines, ignoring the twitch of her lips. She extracted the jewelry from where it now dangled forgotten from his foot. You never could tell. At any moment, he could suddenly remember and pull it apart one bead at a time.

"Who's pretty in their sweater?" The bird cocked his head at her.

"I only said that to make you feel better that you didn't have any feathers," she muttered darkly. "If I'd known I was going to hear it for the rest of your life, I'd have been more careful." Chora gave the macaw a kiss on his beak. Spying the wall clock in the reflection of her dresser mirror, she gave a start. "Oh, shoot, I'd better get changed." She placed the bird on the floor where he hopped off, muttering manically to himself about trains and breakfast cereal. Fondly, she watched him walk over to where one of the cats was sleeping in a basket of washing waiting to be folded before perching himself as a self-appointed, preening sentry. Chora smiled to herself, suddenly not worried about the date. No matter what happened tonight, she would be coming home to these critters, and nothing was ever going to change that.

EVERYWHERE OVERGROOMED and preened women sat. Sometimes in little groups, occasionally with a much older, rotund, balding man. The display of shiny wealth burdened on grotesquely vulgar. Landon shuddered at what his grandparents would make of it all, but determinedly continued to scan the crowd, praying that it would suit his purposes today. He pictured the brassy blonde he'd selected with the fawning aid of the matchmaker. There had been a doll-like plastic hardness to her visage as she smiled—or at least that's what he assumed she'd been doing. It was hard to tell from her over-plumped lips and blindingly perfect teeth verging on terrifying. She had all the hallmarks of a gold digger, and that made her perfect for his needs.

Landon took another sip of his iced water, wishing he was back in Crete continuing with his work at the archaeological dig there. The tantalizing glimpses of a lost civilization he'd been able to glean were only the tip of the iceberg and he should be there, not here on a fishing expedition. His mind was lost in a swirl of elegant dark-haired women dancing with snakes and agile youths leaping over wild-eyed bulls.

"Excuse me?" A gorgeous honey blonde smiled warmly, if a little hesitantly, as she stood looking down at him. "Are you Landon Astley?" He took in her heart-shaped face and glowing, fresh complexion, shown off to perfection by her brightly patterned dress. No need for over-the-top makeup. She was quite simply refreshingly beautiful to behold in the way a daffodil left one with a warm glow of happiness. This bewitching creature looked night and day from what had been presented to him in her picture.

Generations of superior British breeding came to his rescue and he rose, hand extended. "I am, and you are Christina?" Even the name seemed somehow ill-fitting.

For a moment, her smile dimmed ever so slightly and then returned to its former wattage. "I am. May I join you?"

∾

THE WAY he said Christina in his crisply cut-glass tones of old English money had her wondering what her name would sound like on his lips. She didn't remember Christina mentioning that the guy was English. It probably hadn't mattered to her as long as he was a billionaire. Gracefully, she slid into the chair that he held out for her, stealthily peeking at him from under lowered lashes. *The man is a god— if a marble sculpted god had a couple of days' worth of stubble adorning his chiseled jaw!* Chora found herself on the receiving end of a coolly appraising gaze. *Right, I'm here to do a job.*

"I must say, it's a pleasure to make your acquaintance." His lips had a sensuality that seemed at odds with the very properness of his speech. *Why would a man who looks like this and is a billionaire to boot need the services of a matchmaker? Seriously, women should be lining up around the block to get their hands on him.* Chora remembered Christina very much planning on sinking her claws into him. It made her feel strangely relieved to know that he'd escaped her clutches.

"Thank you." Chora took a sip of her water, feeling completely out of her depths. "I'm a little nervous. This is my first date for the matchmaker."

"It's mine, too."

Grabbing hold of the conversational lifeline he'd thrown her, she smiled at him. "I am kinda wondering why you need help with getting dates."

Those eyes stared back at her. It was unnerving. She could capture no hint of what he might be thinking in their cool hazel depths. "Because I have very particular requirements."

Chora felt a spike of alarm. Had she wandered into a Fifty Shades of Grey type of deal here? There was no way she'd signed up for that, thank you very much! She was going to give Christina a piece of her mind when she saw her next. She picked up her purse. "I think there's been some sort of miscommunication here. I'm sure if you contact the match-maker, she will be able to arrange a date with someone who is more suited to your requirements."

Nothing changed in Landon's gaze. There was the slightest furrow of a brow, but he remained coolly composed. "I'm not sure I quite follow."

"Look, I'm not one to judge, but it's not a lifestyle choice that I identify with." Her chair screeched as she resolutely stood. She knew there had to be a catch.

"Are all Americans so confusing?"

"I don't think there's anything confusing about this situation, and it has nothing to do with the fact I'm American," she replied tartly.

"Can you please sit down and hear me out? Then if you're still determined to end our meeting, I'll gladly agree to let the matchmaker know that you were lovely, but unfortunately not my type."

Hesitantly, she resumed her place. "I think I can agree to that."

"I find myself in the challenging position of requiring a wife and neither the inclination nor luxury to do so. In exchange for you agreeing to marrying me in name only and carrying out the charade when in the presence of certain people so they will believe the pretense, I'm willing to give you a great deal of money."

Chora opened and closed her mouth. Had he actually just said what she thought he'd said? She hadn't thought she'd be more horrified than the assumption she'd made just before—which seemed laughable now—but she was. What sort of freakshow had she walked into? A marriage, but not a real marriage, and one that she would get paid for? *No, thank you!*

"I'm not sure I want to know what sort of woman you think I am, but I can tell you I'm definitely not the sort who would take you up on that kind of offer." This time, when she stood, she didn't stop, striding away without a backwards glance at the insulting British billionaire.

Later as Chora emptied out her purse, she could see the funny side of it all. *Misty is going to laugh herself silly when I tell her.* Her fingers brushed something sharp inside. Confused, she extracted a business card with a posh monogram in gold. Elegant handwriting that looked to have been written using a fountain pen was on the other side.

In case you change your mind.

L.A.

Chora threw the card on her side table. *Fat chance about that!*

CHAPTER 4

"What did I ever do to you?" Chora soothed the kitten on her lap that had become startled at the vigor of her delivery.

Christina gave her a quizzical look—at least, Chora thought that was what she was on the receiving end of. It was hard to tell with all the Botox the other woman had. "Today? Or in general?" Chora blinked, thrown off by the response. She had not been expecting that at all. Christina cackled. "Just messing with you."

"Oh." Chora shook her head. "Anyway, that guy you made me go on a date with last night—that guy was next level out of line."

"Wasn't he rich?"

"Ah, I assume so. I mean, yeah, I think he was—is."

Understanding flickered in Christina's otherwise expressionless face. "Oh, old and ugly? A little bit of a belly? I thought he looked too good to be true in the photo." She grabbed at her flat stomach. "Honestly, in this town, everyone's picture has been photoshopped."

Chora gawked at her. *What was she talking about?* The man

she'd met last night most definitely did not need any help. Sure, she hadn't seen what was under the clothing, but she suspected it wasn't going to be flabby. "No, it wasn't anything like that at all."

"Then what's the problem?"

"He wants to pay me to marry him!" Chora returned the kitten to its mother and stood, brushing her hands off. "A total stranger thinks it's okay to try and buy me!" she hissed.

Christina sighed, dramatically dabbing at her nose with a tissue. "Just my luck that I had to get a head cold, otherwise it would've been me he was proposing to. Why does this always happen to me? So, what did you say?"

A twitch began to form in Chora's left eye. *What was wrong with this woman?* "I told him exactly what he could do with his offer, and it wasn't in a friendly way either."

"Wait, you actually knocked him back? Are you insane?"

"Look, you can thank me some other time. But if I remember correctly, you have poo patrol to take care of." Christina gave a little huff, flicking her blonde extensions over her shoulder with her taloned hands before mincing off.

"Chora?" one of the volunteers called from the office. "Can I talk to you?"

Leaving the blonde drama queen to her task, Chora made her way over. "Sure thing, what's happening?"

"Mike, the food supplier, says he won't deliver any more feed until we've paid our bill."

Chora frowned at her. "That's impossible, we've paid our bill. I mean, after the last fundraiser, we could even be in front on payments." She began to fish her phone out of her pocket. "Let me call Rochelle, and she can get to the bottom of it. Thanks for letting me know, but I'm sure it's all just a huge misunderstanding." Finding the bookkeeper's contact, she waited as it rang. Her frown deepened as it went to voicemail. "Hi, Rochelle, it's Chora from Animals Are

Forever. Can you please give me a call back when you get this? Bye." She hung up, tapping the phone thoughtfully against her chin. Inspiration struck. She was pretty sure she had access to the accounting software too, she just never used it, preferring to go over the reports with Rochelle at the end of each month.

Going to her office, she rummaged about until she found her diary from the year earlier in the bottom. Triumphantly she flicked to the last page and found all the details. After logging into the network using the bookkeeper's login, email notifications began to pop up almost immediately. Horrified, she began to open them, each either demanding payment, a final notice, or a notice that services had been suspended. A sense of impending doom suffocated her. *What was going on?*

EMBEZZLED. The word hung in the air between Chora and the kindly police officer. *Every last penny gone.* The officer cleared his throat. "I wish we could do more, Miss Davis, but right now all we can do is follow the leads and try to bring your bookkeeper back to face charges."

The enormity of the situation hit Chora hard. She had a lot of animals depending on her. "But what do I do right now?"

"You go home, and you let us deal with it."

She nodded, knowing it was what he expected. Leaving the police station, she berated herself for being a fool. She'd trusted Rochelle. Heck, the bookkeeper had worked at the charity for five years and had never once given her cause for suspicion.

Later after a shower, Misty's words from the gala fundraiser haunted her. *You'll be financially secure for years. You can help all the animals that need it.* How was she ever going to tell her friend what had happened? Spying the business card on her dresser, she made up her mind. Maybe she didn't have to.

∾

SHE WALKED into the restaurant like a beam of sunlight on a cloudy day illuminating everything that came into her orbit. Landon rose as she approached, holding a chair out and waiting for her to settle herself. The picture of the perfect gentleman. One who needed to buy a bride. It was a role that still rankled him.

"I must admit, I was somewhat surprised to hear from you again." Chora colored under his gaze.

Her beautiful green eyes disappeared under a sweep of dark eyelashes as she fiddled with the napkin in front of her. "I never expected to have to call you. There are a few things I need to tell you."

Interesting. "Go on."

"Um, well, firstly, I'm not actually Christina." She finally raised her eyes to look at him. Landon was surprised to see pleading in their depths. "Christina's an, ah, acquaintance and she got sick and asked me to go on the date with you as a favor because she still wanted to get matches from the matchmaker."

"So, who are you?" *And why are you here now?*

"I'm Chora Davis. I actually run an animal charity called Animals Are Forever. Christina promised it would only be one date and I'd never have to see you again and then you, um … well, you made your offer like you did."

Landon took a sip of chardonnay, never once sparing her from his steely gaze. "And as I remember you were quite indignant and left riding a particularly high horse. Why did you call me to meet?"

"Because I want more details about your offer."

Disappointment soured the wine in his mouth. *She wasn't any different from the rest. Everyone had their price.* "What would you like to know?"

"What exactly are you offering?"

"Marriage in name only, but the charade must be believable. When we are together, we will live under the same roof and you will be expected to attend family events and, at them, play the part of a loving wife. After twelve months, we can quietly go our separate ways, and after a suitable period of time, divorce. It should be no hardship since, during our time together, I anticipate—except for the odd occasion—you will be based here due to your interests, and I will be based in Europe for my work."

"Oh, what do you do?"

"I'm an archaeologist."

"Oh." That seemed to throw her a little. For some reason, it always had that effect when he told people what he did. "You mentioned payment?"

"One million upfront, another ten million when the marriage is over. I think you will agree that it's a very generous offer."

Chora returned to her torture of the napkin. "It is. And no hanky-panky?"

"No hanky-panky." It was reassuring how businesslike she was being about this. Although the thought of hanky-panky with the gorgeous blonde was tempting.

"Why do you need to do this?" Her fingers ceased their restless movement, and this time he found himself on the end of a determined gaze.

"Since my father passed away, I'm next in line to be my grandfather's heir. A condition of receiving my inheritance is that I get married before I turn thirty. Otherwise, it all goes to my uncle. And guess how old I am at my birthday next month."

"Thirty?" She pursed her lush mouth. "I wouldn't think it would be that hard to find someone to marry you. After all, you're a billionaire and look"—she gestured at him—"like that," she finished lamely.

Landon smiled to himself. So, she thought he was attractive. "It is hard to get someone who doesn't have the silly notion that it will end up as more." He sipped his wine again. "I must say, I appreciate how businesslike you are being about this. At least I'm not dealing with a romantic who plans on falling in love."

"Gosh, no. I couldn't think of a worse outcome." *Okay, that stung a little.* "If I agree, what happens next?"

Satisfaction made his lips quirk. "We get married."

CHAPTER 5

"Oh." Chora seemed a little shocked when he'd informed her that they would be married by the end of the week. "I guess there's no point delaying it."

The fact she'd managed to regroup so quickly boded well for their business arrangement. Landon didn't have time for drama. Not when the Minoan mysteries needed to be solved. "My sentiments exactly. We will go somewhere suitable, maybe Venice, unless there's somewhere you would prefer?"

"No." Chora quickly shook her head. "Wherever you think is best."

"Excellent." *Chora was turning out to be an excellent choice.* "An abundance of photos will be taken to capture the happy occasion as proof to show anyone interested in the nuptials."

"Smart."

Landon paused for a moment to assess if she was being facetious or not. Green eyes stared guilelessly back at him. Deciding she wasn't, he nodded his agreement at her assessment. "It's important we cover all bases."

She sucked on her bottom lip as she stared off somewhere

past his right shoulder. *Considering, perhaps?* "And then what?"

"Then I'll purchase somewhere for us to live here and we will move in." Her wide eyes fastened on his. "There's nothing to fret about. As I mentioned previously, I will be away most of the time in Europe for my work. Think about it like this. You will have a place to live in for free for the duration of our marriage."

"I guess there's that."

Landon was beginning to suspect that Chora may still be processing the situation. Her responses seemed rather curt compared to the woman he'd met previously who'd given him an earful.

"Shall we toast our impending marriage?" He flagged down a passing waiter. "A bottle of champagne, please. I trust you will provide something suitable for a momentous occasion." The man gave a single nod of his head and scurried away before returning a few minutes later to fill their glasses, the time having been spent in relative silence.

Landon raised his glass. "To you becoming Lady Astley."

The pale golden liquid came perilously close to spilling from Chora's glass as she stared back at him. "Hey, what?"

Casually, he sipped his champagne. "I thought I mentioned that I'm a lord." He waved it away. "You'll get used to it." From the way she continued to cast worried glances his way, he began to think maybe she wouldn't.

A WEEK of stewing over the decision she'd made and here she was, one flight and a night's sleep away from getting married. At least Chora felt strangely at ease on the private plane, since she'd spent many a trip flying to a gala with Misty on hers.

"This is for you." Chora jerked in surprise as Landon placed a folder on the table in front of her. "I will require you to read it and memorize its contents. Also, that you supply me with one similar about you before we return from our wedding."

Curiously, she opened it. It was filled with information about Landon's life. His birthday, job—archaeologist specializing in the Minoan Culture and based in Crete—and where he went to school—Eton and Oxford, thank you very much. There were even little notes about where they met. None of it really described him as a person or gave a hint to what was behind that upper crust British exterior. It was all rather cold and soulless.

"I'll make sure I do."

"Excellent. I look forward to perusing your file. Chora?" Landon looked over, those hazel eyes drilling into her, making her heart beat a little unsteadily.

"Yes?"

"I do believe that this year won't be a hardship for you."

It might not be a hardship, but what was normal about marrying a stranger in name only? Not trusting herself to speak, she nodded and fixed her attention on the packet of information in front of her. A lot of facts, but not one single clue as to who the man really was.

GRITTY-EYED, Chora rolled over and checked the time on her phone. *Only a couple of hours till the big "I do".* She'd spent the night in the luxurious suite overlooking the Venetian Grand Canal thinking about the man she was about to marry. He was a little brisker than she was used to, but then again, she'd never met a British lord before, so maybe it was just a cultural thing. He didn't seem to suffer from an overabundance of emotion, which might be a good thing. At least she wouldn't be living on the edge of her seat when he was around. *What if he was a serial murderer under that proper exterior and this was his MO?*

A knock on the door sent her scrambling to hide under the covers, her imagination taking hold. "Who is it?"

"My name is Mimi, and Landon has asked me to help you select something suitable to wear today." The woman's voice had a wonderful Italian cadence. Deciding she was being silly, she uncovered herself and shuffled over. Self-consciously, she answered the door to a stranger with unbrushed hair and teeth and still in her pajamas. To make matters worse, the statuesque woman with the clothing rack standing on the other side was stunning. *How did Landon know this woman?*

With the barest raise of a brow, Mimi sauntered in like a queen, her clothing rack trundling behind her. "I wasn't expecting anyone," offered Chora. "Um, if you give me a few minutes, I'll have a shower and we can get started, I guess."

Mimi looked her up and down before nodding. It was hard to not feel judged and slightly jealous at how put together the other woman was. *But hey, wasn't that a good sign if she was here to help with my fashion sense?* The hot water washed away the last of Chora's fatigue. Maybe she wasn't quite ready for whatever the day was going to bring, but she was as ready as she was ever going to be.

Slipping on a pair of sweats, she took a deep breath and prepared to enter the battlefield. Chora rocked back on her heels when she saw that Mimi had her suitcase open and was rummaging through the contents. "Can I help you with anything?"

"No." Mimi answered completely unfussed. "It is a good thing Landon insisted I be here today. Is this what you had thought to wear?" The Italian woman held up the simple white slip dress Chora had packed between disdainful fingers.

Chora snatched if from her hands, clutching it defensively to her chest. "It was all I had, and it wasn't like Landon gave me much time to find anything else. Heck, it was barely enough time to get someone to cover at the charity for me and feed my animals..." She trailed off, afraid she would start crying. Suddenly she seemed a long way from everything she loved. *Maybe this was a mistake.* And then she thought of the animals. There was no way she was going to let them down, and Landon had assured her it would barely change her life at all.

Mimi's face softened a fraction. "Bella, that is why I am here. To make sure you don't hide your beauty in something that is not worthy of you. Together we will send you out to your wedding day looking like a princess."

"Or a lady, at least. Landon's a lord, isn't he?"

"Currently he is a marquess, and his grandfather is a duke. But you are right, my little American, we need to make you look like a marchioness." *Marchioness Chora,* she smothered a giggle. *I wonder if I can get Misty to call me that.*

Mimi's eyes narrowed as she surveyed what she had to work with. You have some curves, but not too much, but such an elegant neck."

Chora's hand flew to touch the body part that had just been complimented. *Didn't a neck just keep your head from falling onto your shoulders?* "Um, thanks, I think."

"It does not have to be too formal as it is an elopement, but still, it must be modest as you will be having it at St Mark's Basilica." Mimi began to hum as she slid the dresses along, the hangers clicking as they reached their destination. Chora wasn't sure what was the discard pile and what wasn't.

"Is that special? To get married there, I mean."

"It is the Cathedral of Venice. There is no more special

church to be married in all of Venice." Mimi pulled out a slinky mermaid cut dress, her mouth pursed as she considered. "No, that is not the silhouette we want." She returned it back to its mates and with a decisive flick, moved it to the right. *So, that's where the rejects go.* "This—this is the one." Reverently, the Italian woman held the gown out.

She was right. From the delicate lace cap sleeves to the way the same pale lace draped into loose folds in the skirt, it was demure. But with a dramatic neckline that created the right amount of drama, it was perfect. Wistfully, she stared at it. This might be the only wedding she ever had, but at least she had the chance to wear this beautiful dress. *Even if nothing else was real.*

EVEN WHEN HE had been a little boy, there had been something about the serenity of religious sites that always held Landon in its sway whenever he found himself in one. Waiting for his bride to make an appearance under the Greek marble columns of the niche, he permitted himself a smug smile. He'd done it. He'd outsmarted his cold, calculating grandfather. *And Chora was being a jolly good sport about it all, too.*

"Son?" The father put his hand on Landon's shoulder, calmly looking toward the end of the crypt. Landon followed the man of God's gaze.

There was something in the way Chora walked. He'd noticed it when he'd first met her, and since the short time Landon had known her, he'd never failed to take pause to admire her entrance. There was a joyousness to her movements, a grace at simply being alive and in the moment. *Maybe it was an American thing. It most definitely wasn't a British thing. At least not in his inner circle.* She was nothing like the drab society belles who had always been in his orbit. Chora's clear gaze fastened on him as she made her way over, the simple elegance of her lace dress breathtaking. The irony struck him that it would be a lucky man who could call such a woman his, and very soon that honor would be Landon's, if only in name.

As Chora listened to the father speak about what their life together should entail, her light seemed to dim. *Maybe she was feeling jetlagged from the trip over.* She rose in his estimations. *Such a trooper.*

Landon's sense of satisfaction peaked as he said his "I do". Soon there would be nothing in the way of him getting his inheritance and continuing to devote himself to the Minoan mysteries that called to him. He gently held her quaking hand as he slid the diamond-encrusted platinum band home on her finger and tried to silently lend her his support. This might be a marriage in name only, but that didn't mean he was a monster.

If Chora's voice shook a little as she struggled through his lengthy name and title, then she was perhaps approaching the end of her endurance. Patiently, he waited as her trembling made it difficult to place his wedding ring on the correct finger. A nervous giggle of relief escaped her when it finally made its way on.

"You may kiss the bride."

Landon swallowed. He wasn't an idiot, but somehow he'd forgotten this part of the ceremony would take place. Chora stared back at him, her tongue darting nervously along her bottom lip. He was dimly aware of the photographer he'd arranged to capture the happy moment getting into prime position for the money shot. *It was one little kiss. How hard could it be to be convincingly in love?* Pep talk over, he slowly leaned in. *One little kiss, that's all.*

~

"I didn't know if you were going to run away or faint when the father said to kiss me." Chora laughed, well onto her third glass of celebratory champagne back at the hotel, this time in a shared honeymoon suite. "You have kissed a girl before, right?"

"Yes." She really did have the most infectious sense of humor. "I'm actually quite experienced, I'll have you know, but I've never kissed my wife before." *There it was again—wife.* He didn't know whether he wanted to damn the old man for forcing him into this position or enjoy the ride. Landon hadn't expected the kiss to linger on his mind afterwards. Her lips had been softly yielding against his, even if she'd been a little tense in his arms. And then, just like a willow in the breeze, she'd molded herself to him.

"I wonder if you look so terrified in the photos, or if I look as awkward as I felt." Chora appeared to be feeling the effects of her drink, slowly blinking at him.

"I rather think you'll find you looked beautiful." He hadn't planned on giving her the compliment, but it felt nice to do it just the same.

Chora smiled brightly at him. "Aw, you're just a big teddy bear under all that British stiff upper lip, aren't you?" She scrunched up her mouth. "Are we really going to pull this off convincingly? That we're madly in love? I mean, how are you going to explain me to your friends and family?"

It was his turn to take a drink. *It really was a rather good vintage.* "I have three people whom I consider friends, and they already know about the plan. And my family, well, they will be told that we fell madly in love and didn't see the sense in waiting. They'll blame it on my mother's genetics."

Her eyes, although blurry, seemed to see into his soul.

"You don't seem the impulsive type to me, and I've only just met you."

"Neither did my father if you'd met him, and she got him to marry her." *And haven't I spent my life paying for it.*

"I don't really know what that means. All you had in the folder is that he's dead." Why did she keep looking at him like that?

"You haven't given me your folder yet." It was time he steered the conversation away from this line of questioning. The way she slowly blinked while resting her chin on her hand was hypnotic.

"That's because I'm not going to do a folder. I'll just tell you what you need to know, you know, like a verbal story of my life, and then you ask questions and stuff. It'll be more fun that way and, I don't know, maybe we might actually get to know each other." Her chin took on a decidedly mulish tilt.

"I'd prefer the folder. We only need to know each other enough to convince other people. I think it's a bit extreme to put more into it than that."

Chora folded her arms across her chest. "I hear marriage is all about compromise."

"Not the ones I've seen. I think it would be wise to end this discussion and bid you goodnight. I'll take the pull-out sofa." She seemed like she wanted to say more, but Landon wasn't going to be drawn into a tit for tat about what marriage should be. *They blooming weren't even really married and she was already trying to argue and get her own way.* "Goodnight, Chora. You did splendidly today."

"Thank you. It cowas my first time getting pretend married and I think I did rather well, too." If her tone was a little sarcastic, then Landon pretended he didn't notice as he exited the room. *If they keep these jabs up, at least no one would doubt that they really were married.*

CHAPTER 6

*B*oats busily shunted their passengers along the canal as Chora sipped her coffee from a delicate bone china cup. One day she'd like to come back here and really see Venice, not just an airport, a honeymoon suite and the Basilica. Heck, she'd be rich enough after all this was done, maybe she could treat herself. *Who am I kidding? I'd feel guilty if it went on anything other than the animals.*

She breathed in deeply and then out, trying to expel all the doubts that buffeted her as she stared now unseeingly at the vista below. *What have I really gotten myself into?* Landon's comments from the night before didn't really bode well for the time they did need to spend together. It wasn't like she'd suggested they become best friends, but there could at least be some sort of human connection between them. Chora could feel her cheeks flush as she angrily recalled him scoffing at her. *Stupid folder.* The dude really did have a messed-up notion about marriage. She gave a rueful chuckle over the rim of the cup she held poised to her lips. *Says she who had just gotten fake married for money. Ironic much?* She shrugged before finally taking a sip. Maybe she shouldn't judge after all.

Chora turned at the sound of the front door opening, unsure how to greet the damp looking Landon who entered. Somehow, "husband dearest" didn't seem appropriate.

This morning there seemed a relaxed quality to him, a looseness in the way he held himself. Well, until he saw her. "Oh, you're awake, I see."

Chora raised her cup in salute, consciously forcing herself not to grip the delicate handle too hard for fear of breaking it. "And I see you must have been awake quite early to escape."

The tips of his ears reddened under her steady scrutiny. "I was awake early to escape—as you so graciously put it—to make use of the Isopod."

She blinked, not entirely sure what they were talking about anymore. "The Isopod?"

Landon made his way further into the suite and began to pour himself a tea. "Yes. It's an isolation float tank that has incredibly high levels of magnesium in it. When you're in it, it's the closest you can come to a dreamlike state and still be awake. I find it useful for restoring my sense of equilibrium." Chora wondered how he managed to say it all with such a haughty manner.

"Wow, not what I'd expected." She made a pretense of picking up his folder. "Did you put that in here? How awkward if I didn't know that Isopuddles are one of your passions."

"Isopod."

"What?" Chora stared blankly at him.

"It's an Isopod, not an Isopuddle."

"Same meat, different gravy." She waved away the correction, almost spilling her coffee in the process. "You know, I'm thinking you'd fit in perfectly in LA."

Landon's eyes narrowed as he turned to fully face her, teacup and saucer held in hand as if it were the most natural thing in the world. "I'd rather die." Horror laced every toffy word uttered.

Chora felt tired. This might not be a real marriage, but she didn't need to nettle him either. She gave him an apologetic smile. "I'm sorry, I don't mean to start today off on the wrong foot. I'm a little on edge, I guess." She sat down on the sofa, facing out toward the large French doors she'd been standing in front of. Somehow the airy lightness kept her fears at bay. "So, what happens next?"

"I'll leave from here to return to my work in Crete. There's no sense in me returning to LA just to fly back again."

"Of course." Why did it feel like he was abandoning her as quickly as possible? And why wasn't she relieved?

"I've taken the liberty of arranging a property to be purchased in Beverly Hills. It has substantial grounds and should be suitable for your needs." Landon sipped on his tea, studiously endeavoring not to make eye contact with her. "Although it is furnished, I've had your belongings moved over."

Alarmed, Chora stared at him. "What happened to my animals?"

"A bird, rabbits and some cats?"

"Yes, those!" Tense, she was about ready to fly into action.

"They were also relocated. According to the housekeeper, they have made themselves at home. The bird in particular seems fond of destroying things."

Chora let out her pent-up breath, her limbs drooping now that she knew her precious pets were safe. She gave a weak laugh. "Yeah, Mac-attack has been known to destroy a thing or two in his time. To be fair to him, he spent ten years locked in a cage that he couldn't move in at all. When I got him, he was completely bald because he'd plucked out all his feathers due to stress."

"My understanding is that macaws are quite clever birds. Why would someone have one as a pet and not care for them properly?"

"As a species, human beings are the worse. Mac-attack's previous owners thought that it would make them look cool to own one and then they lost interest. Seriously, that partic-ular story applies to so many animals that come into our shelter." Somehow, the room seemed gloomier now, the need to help animals that needed it weighing down on her.

"Then they are very lucky to have someone like you care enough to make a difference." Landon locked eyes with her from across the room, nodding approvingly. "Now, I shall obviously give you some money to make sure things run smoothly. We had discussed a million, will that be sufficient?"

Chora swallowed. She felt dirty discussing money. *That's all this marriage is, remember? It's just a business transaction.* "Yes, that should do."

"If you need more, we can discuss it as the need arises. After all, I don't want the animals to suffer any more than they have."

The fact that Landon cared enough about the animals to make the offer suddenly made him seem a little less coldly reserved. Chora beamed at him, surprised when a hesitant smile graced his lips in reply. "Thank you, but this time, I'm making sure I know where every penny is spent."

"Jolly good. Now, we will meet up once in a while and put on a show of affection, but in general, your life won't change a great deal." *What every newly married woman wants to hear.* A slight edge of hysteria began to creep in. *What had I done?* "Now, if you'll excuse me, I'm leaving this morning to return to work. The plane will take you back to LA this afternoon."

Landon paused on his way to the bathroom door. "I'll be in touch."

The hysteria that had begun to bubble now threatened to explode. With shaky fingers, she picked up Landon's file from the coffee table. *How am I going to be able to explain this?* Flipping through the pages, she desperately looked for any traces of what the real Landon looked like.

~

SURROUNDED by stone walls and terracotta roofed buildings, Landon sipped a local wine as he breathed in the welcomed air of home, safely back in his villa in Archanes. The hills with their olive groves and vineyards wrapped securely around him. Tomorrow he would return to his work at Knossos, but on this balmy evening, it was enough simply to be.

The ring of his phone broke through his enjoyment. Popping a slice of salami into his mouth, he answered. "Hello, chap."

"Did you bloody well go through with it or not?" demanded Alistair. Landon could almost picture him blustering as he paced around. "Tell me you didn't."

"Why would we want him to do that?" Stirling interrupted. *Ah, this was a conference call then.*

"Don't be daft, man, of course Laddy did it," added Freddy. "He's always done what needed to be done." There was a tinge of admiration for their fallen bachelor friend.

"Chaps, I'm a married man now and will remain so for at least a year." Landon noticed a dog skulking about at the edge of the terrace, woefully thin and missing patches of fur.

"How on earth did you manage to convince a woman to marry a mug like you?" Freddy demanded.

"It is quite simply a business transaction." Landon held

out a slice of salami toward the dog. The mutt gave an anxious whine, but came no closer. Judging from the gray around his muzzle, he was no longer in the first flush of puppyhood. "And not a moment too soon. Grandfather has summoned me home to the family estate. He was quite vexed when I informed him I had gotten myself a bride."

He didn't think it was necessary to share with his friends that Grandfather couldn't resist throwing in his face how unsuitable Landon's mother had been. He'd gone so far as to demand to meet Chora with threats about informing his uncle that he would be next in line if she wasn't someone who befitted marrying into the family.

"I'm going to need your help," he continued. "I'll be bringing her over to meet the family soon, and you will all have to assist with making sure she isn't found wanting."

"You know you can bloody well count on us," Alistair vowed. "It might be rather fun."

"You always did like games," grumbled Freddy.

"No, he always liked winning," corrected Stirling. "Now, your blushing bride—what do you really know about her?"

Landon thought about the honey blonde with the sunny smile. "She's an animal charity director." He noticed the dog was no longer there.

"Well, philanthropic work has always been favored by upper class women," Stirling said. "Isn't your grandmother a patron for saving hedgerows?"

"Yes." Landon was already feeling better now that he knew he had the support—albeit teasing support—of his friends. "Chora's quite charming actually. I think she will do quite well with a bit of preparation." He rose and filled a terracotta dish with water and placed it with a handful of salami halfway between him and where he'd last seen the dog.

"Charming, is she?" Mirth boomed down the phone from

Alistair. "Tell me you know more about her than the fact she's charming and has an animal charity."

"She's American," Landon replied defensively, taking a seat again.

"Well, there you go, chaps. Landon knows all he needs to know," Alistair said. "What could possibly go wrong?'

Landon wished his Aussie friend would keep his mocking to himself. Doubts began to raise their ugly heads, sending tendrils of unease snaking through him. *Maybe I should follow up with Chora on her folder.* It was possible that his friend might have a point. *Maybe I need to know more than that my wife is a charming, animal loving American.*

CHAPTER 7

Chora clutched Mr Hoppikins to her chest. "I know this place is a lot bigger than where we used to live." *Understatement of the year.* "But this is home now, and you need to stop getting lost all the time." The manicured lawns and gardens were amazing for the animals and such an improvement on what she'd been able to offer them in her apartment, but they still appeared shellshocked from their new living arrangements. *Maybe we all are.*

"Is the bunny all right, Chora?" the housekeeper, Dorothy, asked, concern making her kindly face wrinkle. "He's such a sweetie. I'd hate for something to happen to him."

Chora liked the older woman and, luckily, she was an animal lover too. Good thing, considering the menagerie she had to tolerate in her spotless domain. Chora was still getting used to the idea of having someone in the house taking care of everything. *Oh, who am I kidding? I'm getting used to this situation full stop.*

Returning from Venice without Landon, she had immersed herself in his folder, trying to get an insight into the British enigma that she was tied to for the next twelve months. Today was the first day she was returning back to work. With a final kiss, she handed the escape artist over to Dorothy. "I think it might be best if he spends some time in his hutch while I'm at work, just to be on the safe side. And I apologize in advance for anything Mac-attack might say. He usually doesn't mean any of it." The housekeeper gave a low laugh as she nodded. Picking up her handbag from the counter, Chora waved goodbye to her animals. It was time to see what havoc a week away from the shelter had wrought.

Pushing the door open into her office, she was surprised to see Christina with her feet up on her desk, glued to her phone. Annoyed, she pushed the other woman's feet off. "Hey!" A startled Christina scowled, looking for who to unleash her anger at. "Oh, it's you, Chora. I didn't expect you back so soon."

"I don't remember telling you when to expect me back, or that you could use my office while I was away, for that matter."

Huffily, Christina removed herself from behind Chora's desk. "Well, I didn't think you'd mind. Where'd you go, anyway?"

The ring of her phone saved Chora from having to answer. Surprise and more than a hint of anticipation spliced through her when she saw it was Landon. "Hello?"

"Hello, Chora. I trust you are comfortably moved into the new property?" His voice was always so perfectly urbane. *I wonder what he sounds like when he's mad and thinks no one is around?*

"I am, thank you." She wasn't really sure what else to add. Making small talk with her husband was proving more diffi-cult than she'd imagined. Noticing Christina was still in the room, she waved her toward the door. Sullenly, the other woman skulked off, if only to the other side of the threshold.

"Excellent. And the weather has been fine?" *Really? Now*

we're discussing the weather.

"Yes, it's been lovely. But it is California, after all. And how about where you are?"

"Glorious sun-drenched days here in Crete." *Who'd have thought that proper Landon would utter such a romantic description?* Chora couldn't help but feel a little jealous of the love he obviously had for the island. "I'm calling because I'm going to need you to come to England next week."

"But I only just got back," Chora protested as she shut the door firmly on the lingering Christina. "I can't just drop everything whenever you decide you need me."

"I understand, and I hope you know I wouldn't intrude if it wasn't absolutely imperative. It was, however, part of our little business arrangement that you would play the part of a doting wife when required, and this is one of those instances." There was a firmness to his voice, a silken strength that was hugely attractive. Chora tried to ignore the warmth flushing through her veins. "My grandfather insists on meeting you. I can't tell you enough just how important it is for you—for us—to be convincing. One would rather not fall at the first hurdle, after all."

"I see." A knot twisted in her belly. She knew she was going to have to convince people. Heck, that was the whole point of this fake marriage. But now being faced with it, she felt ill. *What happens if I can't do it?* She knew the answer to her own question, Landon wouldn't get his inheritance and she wouldn't get her money and then she'd be back at square one and struggling to keep the animal shelter afloat. "How long will I be required?"

"A few weeks at most, I imagine. We need people to have no doubts whatsoever that our relationship is real." *Piece of cake.* "On that matter, I still require your folder."

"I've only just gotten home, and I thought we'd agreed to a verbal presentation."

"No, you suggested, and I declined. I deal much better with facts I can read." There was that firmness again.

Chora sighed. *What did it matter anyway?* "Fine, when I get a chance, I'll throw something together. When do you need me in sunny old England?"

"Wednesday."

She almost dropped the phone. "This week?" she squeaked.

"Yes."

"But it's already Monday." *What universe did this man live in that it seemed perfectly normal for someone to just pop over to England with a few days' notice?*

"Obviously, I'll send the jet for you." *Obviously.* She rolled her eyes so loudly she was surprised he couldn't hear it through the phone.

"Well, that makes all the difference," Chora said, sarcasm lacing heavily through her words. "Look, I need to go. I now have a lot of things I need to get organized and not much time to do it."

"Don't worry about organizing too much for your trip. Most of it can be taken care of once you're here."

Frustrated, she considered smacking her forehead, but thought better of it. "Yeah, I was talking about all the things that need to be done here, for my charity. Send through the details of the flight, and if I get a chance, I'll email some personal information."

Before he could answer she hung up the phone. The office now felt stuffy. In need of fresh air, she threw open the door, taking a step back when Christina almost bowled her over as she fell in.

"Aren't you the naughty little minx?" The blonde woman gave her a conspiratorial smile. "I assumed like everyone else you were off doing fundraiser things for the charity, but you were with a man, weren't you?"

"Most children know it's not nice to eavesdrop."

"I couldn't help overhearing it while I waited for your phone call to end so I could ask if you wanted me to get you a coffee. Remember, it was part of our deal for you going on that date?"

Chora was beginning to feel like she was drowning in deals she'd made. "That's the excuse you're going with?"

Christina stared innocently back at her. "It's the truth." She perched herself on the edge of Chora's desk and raised her eyebrows at her, her overly filled mouth pursed. "Now, spill."

Chora sighed. She just wanted to be left alone, she had so much to get done and so little time to do it in. "Okay, if I tell you, will you promise that I won't see you for the rest of the day?"

"Of course."

"The short version is this. You know the billionaire I went on the date with?"

"The one I was meant to go on?"

"Yes, that one. Well, the reason I was away was because we got married."

If looks could kill, Chora should've been dead thrice over from the filthy glare Christina threw her way. "Excuse me?"

"Look, he needed to get married, that's why he was with the matchmaker."

"You married a billionaire," Christina said slowly. "MY BILLIONAIRE!" she screeched as it sunk in. "You stole my billionaire!"

Chora rocked back on her heels, shocked at the onslaught from the other woman. She held her hands defensively out in front of her. "No, it's nothing like that. It's not a proper marriage, just on paper. And in a year, it will all be over."

"But for that year, you get all the benefits of marrying a billionaire—and I imagine there will be perks when you divorce as well." Loathing made the blonde woman's features hard. "Tell me how that's supposed to make me feel better."

Clearly, they had very different views on what was important in life. *Who am I to judge? I agreed because I needed the money. Does that make me any better than her?* "Look, it wasn't a planned thing. You're the one who begged me to go."

"That was before I knew he would marry just anyone. Clearly he didn't have standards if he married you."

Ouch. "Well, it's done now, and you're still with the matchmaker, so there's still a chance you'll end up with a billionaire too."

Christina satisfied herself with a final glare. "You better hope so, and it better not be some lousy millionaire."

"I'm sure you'll have more offers than you can handle."

"That's true. If you managed to hook one, imagine what someone like me can catch."

Chora shuddered internally. She didn't want to think about all the things Christina had the potential to catch. "That's right."

Somewhat mollified, Christina stood. "Do you want me to get you a coffee?"

Chora wasn't sure she trusted what she would do to her drink given her current mood. "I'm okay, thanks."

"Well, I'm taking a break. I'll be back once I've gotten my nails done."

With a flick of bleached hair, she was gone. It was days like this that made Chora wonder why Christina volunteered at the charity. Maybe she needed all the karma points she could get. Or maybe it was court ordered. *No.* She chuckled to herself. *I'd know if it was.* Shaking her head at the enigma that was Christina, she closed her office door behind her and went in search of her shelter manager. That was a riddle for another day.

THE RICH TIMBER paneling in the room gleamed, reflecting the light of the room back at Landon from where he sat at his desk. Spread across its varnished surface were all the notes he'd made over his years of study of the Linear A script. His first love would always be his work at archaeological sites, but this puzzle nagged at him, and every few months he found himself pouring over it again, endeavoring to be the first one to translate the ancient Minoan writings.

Today, he couldn't focus. Frustrated, he paced to the wide window overlooking the plane tree lined avenue outside. It was quiet in the way only the extremely affluent could afford in London, birdsongs coming from somewhere in the privet hedge bordering the mansion. Landon raked his fingers through his hair. *I know it's right there staring at me. Focus.* He closed his eyes and drew in a deep breath, but the inner enlightenment he sought evaded him.

"Sir?"

Landon remained focused on the world outside his library. "Yes, Winston?"

"A package has been delivered for you." The butler held out a silver tray, the aforementioned item on it. "Would you like me to place it on your desk?"

"No, I'll take it. Thank you, Winston." Finally, Landon turned and held his hand out. *What was the likelihood it held some missing clue to his Minoan mystery?* The butler handed it over and discreetly left him to it. Picking up a gold letter opener, he sliced open the top of it and extracted a colorful scrapbook, the exterior of it covered in photos and flowing decorations. A closer inspection revealed some of them had Chora at various ages. Curious, he opened it and began to read. *The Minoan mysteries could wait.*

CHAPTER 8

*H*eathrow Airport looked big enough to be its own city from the air. Chora stretched. Even with the splendid luxury of a private plane, it had still been a long flight. Especially given she'd only just returned from one to Venice not so long ago. *Our wedding and the last time I've seen him.* Chora's stomach twisted into knots of anticipation. A man she called her husband and yet barely knew would be waiting for her when she landed. It had surprised her enormously when he'd informed her that he would be collecting her from the airport. *Can't have people think we aren't madly in love now, can we?*

She felt a dropping sensation in her belly, then there was a bounce and the roar of the engines as the pilot rapidly decreased the speed of the plane. Chora had officially made it to England. It was daunting, there's no two ways about it. In Venice it had been neutral territory, but here it was Landon's home ground. Not only was she an outsider, but one whose every move was going to be scrutinized. She had to be one hundred percent on her game. No, she had to be more than that. She had to be convincingly in love.

Taking a deep breath, she unbuckled her seatbelt and made her way down the aisle, smiling at the hostess on the way out. A misting rain made everything seem somehow grayer, and then she saw him leaning against a hunter green Aston Martin, an enormous bunch of flowers in hand. Surprised, she blinked, a warmth fluttering to life inside her —one that she quickly dampened. *None of this is real. We're just actors.* Plastering a smile on her face, she made a show of rushing down the stairs and across the tarmac, Landon meeting her halfway. He gathered her in his arms, kissing the top of her head before handing over the flowers. *Do we look like lovers who have been parted?*

Chora breathed in the heavenly scent of the roses. "English roses from a genuine English man. There's something almost poetic about that."

"I am many things, but always a gentleman." From the way he looked at her, she believed him. "I trust the flight was tolerable?"

Tolerable? Tolerable was flying economy and not having someone in the seat beside you. Being the sole passenger on a private plane was pure heaven. "I managed."

"Excellent." He held open the passenger door for her and Chora slid in, conscious that her slightly damp clothes left a mark on the pristine leather of her seat. Chora looked up to apologize, but Landon had already shut the door on any comment she may have felt the need to make. Awkwardly, she fumbled with her seatbelt as Landon took his place in the driver's seat and drove the car out through the security gates.

Small talk, Chora. Try to think of something to say. "Um, so the weather's a bit gloomy."

Landon scanned the traffic before pulling out. Chora gave a little shriek as she watched oncoming traffic, convinced she was going to die. For his part, Landon was looking entirely the wrong way. It was only once they were out in the traffic that, feeling foolish, she remembered that people drove on the other side of the road in England to what they did in LA. Satisfied that he could take his eyes off the road, Landon gave her a bemused look.

"So gloomy that it's as frightening as you are making it out to be, or does my driving give you cause for concern?"

"Yes, I mean no, neither. I was just a little startled."

"By the weather?"

"No, by your driving. I mean, not by your driving. Just that it's on the wrong side of the road. Well, not wrong here, but back home. But we're not back home, so I guess it's fine." *I sound like an idiot. No one's going to believe we're head over heels in love.* "I don't think this is going to work."

Landon's aristocratic profile crinkled. "Are we still talking about my driving and the weather?"

"No. I'm talking about us. Well, there really is no us, and honestly, I don't think anyone will believe there's an us anyway." Landon nodded as he listened. Relieved that he agreed, Chora relaxed a little. *We were stupid to think it would work anyway.*

"That's why I have a plan."

Chora gaped at him. "A plan?"

"Yes." Smug superiority oozed from every impeccably bred pore. "This week we will practice pretending. My grandparents aren't expecting us until the weekend, and that should give us sufficient time to make this charade believable."

She had to give it to him, the man wasn't a quitter. She wasn't so sure how confident she felt about it all, however. "A week's not that long."

"It's adequate for what we need." He slowed down at a security hut and slowly wound his window down. A police officer walked out of the security hut and tipped his hat. "Good afternoon, Lord Astley."

"Good afternoon."

The bollards that had been blocking the road miraculously disappeared, sinking below ground level. "Have a lovely evening."

And without further ado, the sleek car was once again in motion, this time down an avenue lined with plane trees and privet hedges and old-fashioned lampposts that could have come straight out of a fairytale. Except for the immense stucco mansions, there was nothing overtly ostentatious about the quiet street. At least not by LA standards. It was all frightfully reserved with glistening cream paint, shining green and black railings and vast, expansive buildings with too many windows to count.

Chora could only stare at the display of old wealth as Landon turned into a drive, the black and brass rail gate swinging open before pulling up in front of a creamy white mansion, a formally dressed man in a white shirt and black waistcoat greeting them.

"Winston, this is Lady Astley, my new wife. If you could take her luggage to the master bedroom," Landon said, coming around, his hand held out for Chora as she excited the car. All she could manage was a quick smile before the fellow efficiently set to work. "Chora, Winston is my butler here and is at your disposal."

She wasn't sure what exactly a butler did and wisely remained silent as they entered the grand wooden doors into the foyer. Everything looked like it belonged to the Victorian era at the very least. "I'll remember that."

"If you'll come with me, I'll show you to the master suite for you to freshen up." He led her up a grand curved staircase, past doors and corridors until, at last, he pushed open a door. Winston, hot on their heels, deposited her luggage in a little room to one side before making a dignified exit, closing the door behind him.

It was clear that this was Landon's room. Everywhere was dark aged timber, hunting prints and what looked to be pictures of him on archaeological digs. Uncertainly, she stared at her husband, recalling very clearly him saying there would be no hanky-panky.

"Landon, I think you've made a mistake." It was best he knew that she wasn't going to bend the rules for him, no matter how good-looking he was.

"I think I know what you're going to say."

She raised a brow at him in a challenge. "Really?"

"Yes, and I know this appears slightly forward, but I can't take any chances that something will be passed on to my grandfather. It won't look good if, as newlyweds who have just been reunited, we choose to sleep in separate bedrooms. In a few years maybe, but by then, well, it won't be a concern." He seemed to allow himself a slight smile. At what, Chora wasn't quite sure about.

"Who would say anything?"

"Winston, for one. He trained under my grandparents' butler at their country estate before coming to work for me. I'm never quite sure where his loyalties lie, and I'm not sure I want to test it now."

It seemed a sad way to live, unsure if you could trust someone sharing the same roof with you or living side by side, as it were. "That seems prudent."

Relief softened the tightness around his eyes. Maybe he wasn't as confident as he appeared. "I'm glad you agree. Although we will be sharing this room, I can assure you that I will be taking the couch once we have retired for the night and will clear away the evidence in the morning before Winston comes to set the room straight. No one will be the wiser."

"Are you sure you'll be comfortable?" Chora eyed the low back, two-seater leather sofa doubtfully.

"It's not ideal, I'll grant you. However, I think it's the best we can do in this situation." He glanced around the room as if to give it a final check. "Now, if you'll excuse me, I have some work I need to attend to before we go to dinner. I'll leave you to freshen up." Landon half paused as if to say more before giving her a nod and leaving.

Chora sat down on the edge of the bed, bouncing a few times experimentally. *Landon might not sleep well, but I will.* A curious need to giggle overcame her. Maybe she should give Landon a pet name? Help sell the madly in love act a bit. *Cupcake? Lemon drop? Twinky? Snookums?* She shook her head. Maybe she'd think of something when she got to know him more. Rolling her neck, she lifted her suitcase onto the bed. It seemed like forever since she'd changed clothes. Clutching her toiletries bag under her arm, she answered the call of a long hot shower.

LANDON CONCENTRATED on his reflection as he fixed his pewter silk tie, aligning perfectly in the center, the knot laying just so. Chora still had the unique talent of glowing from within. The damp London skies had done little to dim it. He gave a quick glance at his watch. She should be down any minute for their dinner date. Anticipation mingled with dread. *How hard could it be to act like you were madly in love with someone you barely knew?* Her folder had been very much like her—bright, sparkly and full of surprising information. Reading it, he'd questioned why she was still single, until it had dawned on him that she was very much like him in the sense that their work filled their entire world, leaving very little inclination to seek out relationships with the opposite sex. He'd wondered if she'd felt lonely from time to time, wanting to share something from her day like he often found himself feeling.

"I'm ready when you are."

Landon caught sight of Chora standing behind him in the mirror and slowly turned, taking her in. She wore a simple black dress that fell to mid-thigh with a high neckline and tan-colored fringed booties loudly proclaiming her cowgirl heritage. A leopard print scarf draped around her neck completed the outfit. Her honey blonde hair was in a simple updo, loose strands delicately framing her face, her green eyes striking against the smoky makeup. There was nothing of a fragile English rose to her. She was one hundred percent cactus flower, a striking contrast between strength and bold beauty.

"I'll bring the car around."

Chora appeared startled at his suggestion. Didn't American gentlemen do that? "You don't need to do that. I can just come with you."

His grandmother would have conniptions at the mere suggestion. "If you'd like." Landon offered her his arm, and after a moment's hesitation, she accepted with a smile. Chora was prone to smiling, he noticed. But when one smiled like she did—naturally and with her entire being—that was to be expected, he guessed.

He led her past the Mini Cooper, the Porsche and the Range Rover Sport and to the Aston Martin he'd collected Chora from Heathrow in earlier. Normally when Landon was in Crete, he got around in a battered old ex-military jeep. It was nice to have a little power and speed when he was in London. Just to mix it up, of course. Reaching the car, he held the passenger door open expectantly for his date—correction, wife—enjoying the light jasmine fragrance she wore as it wafted up to him when she slid in. He found a lightness to his step as he made his way over to the driver's side. *She smells like she looks.*

As he pulled away from the house and through security, Chora remained silent, intently staring out the window. "I thought you might like to dine at my club tonight," he said.

She turned, bemused, to look at him. "Like a nightclub?"

"No, a members' club."

"Oh."

"Don't they have them in the States?"

Chora pursed her lips and looked upwards, thinking. "They might," she admitted. "But I've never really heard of them or been to one."

"Well, Lady Astley, you won't be able to say that for much longer." Landon pulled the car up in front of an expectantly waiting valet.

"I keep looking around for some woman who looks like she belongs in Pride and Prejudice." Chora's smile was mischievous. Like a little girl who had just shared a secret. Landon had never realized before that one person could have so many different types of smiles.

"Well, that's what you are. You're a marchioness now through marriage." He stepped out of the car and handed the keys to the attendant. With swift, sure steps, he collected his wife. "Before we meet with my grandparents, we may have to go over how you behave to people of different rank," he said, bending toward her ear to make sure she was the only one who heard it.

"Will there be a test?" Her eyes sparkled.

"Meeting my grandfather will be testing enough." Landon led Chora into the Mayfield Townhouse. He waved at people he knew, gradually becoming aware of the stuffy looks being cast toward his wife. A waiter showed them to a table, and he held the chair for Chora, then settled into one himself.

"This place is ... different." Chora's voice was subdued.

"In what way?" He looked around at the timeless, traditional décor, trying to see what she saw.

"The patterns are somewhat jarring. I mean, the stripes on the floor, and the floral motifs on the wallpaper and then mermaid scale print for the chairs. It's just really clashing. Also, they seem very fond of moss green, British green, red and brown."

"Yes, this club is renowned for having members from the upper echelon of society, and they want them to be comfortable."

"I'm not usually one to worry about things like this, but are people staring at me?" Chora's smile didn't quite reach her eyes this time. Subtly, he surveyed the room, seeing disdain and judgmental glances being sent their way. *No, Chora's way.* "Since you didn't immediately deny it, I take it they are. Why?" She took a sip of water from her glass.

"I don't really have any idea. It may just be that they don't know you. In society, you'll find that everyone knows everyone and have all their lives." Somehow it didn't feel like that was the reason.

"Excuse me." An attendant appeared, hovering at Landon's elbow. "But I'll have to ask you both to leave."

Chora looked horrified, a flush creeping along her cheekbones as she sunk lower in her chair. "Don't be ridiculous," Landon said dismissively, continuing to peruse the menu. "Do you know who I am?"

"Yes, Lord Astley, I do. But I regret that I still need to ask you to leave. The lady accompanying you isn't dressed suitably."

Landon raised a brow in aristocratic challenge. "The lady you refer to is my wife, Lady Astley."

The waiter cleared his throat uncomfortably. "I beg your pardon, Lady Astley. However, your footwear doesn't comply with our dress code."

Chora swiveled to stare down in confusion at the offending part of her attire. Face scrunched, she looked up. "I don't understand."

"The dress code clearly states no casual boots or cowboy boots." The man's patronizing tone coupled with his smug visage was beginning to annoy Landon.

"But they aren't cowboy boots," disagreed Chora. "They're booties, you know, ankle boots. Sure, they have some fringe on them, but that doesn't make them cowboy boots."

"My lovely wife is, as you can tell, American and I believe, out of the three of us, the more knowledgeable about what is and is not a cowboy boot. Would you not agree?" Landon made a show of being bored with the conversation.

"Lord Astley, they look like cowboy boots to the management of this club. May I once again request that you leave and return in more suitable attire."

"Landon." Chora reached out and gently clasped his forearm where it lay on the table. "It's not worth it. Let's just go."

Giving the haughty attendant one final glare, Landon rose and held his hand out to Chora. "The food here isn't that well rated anyway." Ignoring the whispers and horrified enjoyment of his peers, he strode from the room. He was still gnawing over what had happened when the valet drove up in his car. Their very first outing in front of London's elite and this was how it ended. He gripped the steering wheel.

"I'm sorry, Landon," Chora said softly, misery stamped over her features, her smile vanquished.

"Maybe next time you can manage to wear something suitable." Landon didn't mean to be so coldly cutting to her—after all, she hadn't really done anything wrong—but anxious bitterness twisted his words into harshness.

"Well, if you knew they weren't suitable, why didn't you say anything when we were at the house? Then I could've changed them. If this doesn't work, it's as much your fault as mine"

Her words hit closer to home than he cared to admit. *What happens if this doesn't work?* Landon's mouth pressed into a thin line. One that didn't change once they returned home, and both went to bed in silence. Long into the night, uncomfortable on his couch, he stared at the ceiling. *This had to work. There were no other options.*

CHAPTER 9

*E*arly morning had always been the time of day that Chora cherished the most. The day still held endless opportunities and was fresh and new. This morning she lingered in Landon's large bed, aware that everything in the room was his. A feeling of disgruntlement held her firm in its grasp, a deep sense of discontentment lingering from the events of the previous evening. She'd gone to bed feeling peevish and she'd woken up exactly the same. *Grandma always said you get out of the same side of the bed you went to sleep in.*

Last night, when everyone had been looking down their stuffy noses at her, she'd wanted to cry. But she was made of tougher stuff than that and had marched from the club with her head held high. What she hadn't expected was Landon turning it all back on her, making out like it was her fault. *Some sort of pretend husband he'd turned out to be.* She'd heard him leave the room earlier, but had pretended to sleep, not yet willing to talk to him. Who were they kidding? This wasn't going to work. Wouldn't it be better to call it quits instead of wasting more time and effort on a lost cause?

Chora rubbed the bridge of her nose. *I should probably call and see how everyone is with the animals.* Reaching out to the bedside table, she fumbled for her phone and dialed the shelter's number.

"Hello, Animals Are Forever, Alice speaking."

"Hello, Alice, It's Chora. I'm just dialing in to see how everyone is."

"We miss you, obviously, but it's been busy. A puppy mill just closed down and we've taken in those mama dogs and puppies. We are at full capacity and then some. The mamas either have puppies or are about to. Thank goodness everything got fixed with the pet food delivery because we have a lot of hungry mouths."

Chora's throat tightened as frustration fought with anger. "When will people learn? I mean, if you buy a puppy from a pet store, it's probably from a puppy mill. At least they're in a safe place now."

"They are. I hate to do this, Chora, but the vet is coming to give everyone a check-up and everyone needs to help. Is there anything else?"

"No, Alice, thank you for caring about the animals." She felt useless being an ocean away from where she was really needed.

"No problem."

After her conversation with Alice, she called Dorothy, the housekeeper, who had now been pressed into full-time pet sitter duties. Apparently, Mac-attack kept her company as she did her chores and they watched soap operas together. She'd even found a way to keep the rabbits where they were meant to be. A tinge of sadness crept over Chora that she wasn't being missed by her animals, but at the same time—and this was the bigger part of her—she was glad they were safe and happy. Chora sighed. It was crystal clear she couldn't waltz out and end this charade. The animals needed her to provide for them, and this was the only way she could think of to fix everything. With grim determination, she pushed the covers back and headed to the shower. It was time her and Landon had a little talk.

Feeling refreshed now she was up and in clean clothes, her steps faltered as tantalizing aromas wafted from the dining room. *I guess the talk can wait till after breakfast.*

Silver serving dishes lined the buffet. Curious, she lifted the lids and peeked inside as she made her way down the row—fried eggs, sausages, bacon, cooked tomatoes, mushrooms, baked beans, black pudding and hot buttered toast. This was most definitely not a LA breakfast. Chora found herself approving. It might not be good for her waistline, but her tastebuds were thrilled.

"Lady Astley." Winston appeared, a silver tea tray in hand. "Would you care for tea or coffee?"

"Coffee would be great." Chora smiled at him as she collected a plate and began to pile it up high. It dimmed slightly when she remembered Landon's words yesterday about the butler potentially being a spy for his grandfather. She'd have to be careful. "I overslept this morning, and Landon was already gone. He usually leaves a note, but it must have slipped his mind. Do you know where he is?"

"He's in his study, Lady Astley."

Chora sat down at the long antique table where the day's newspapers had been laid out. "I'll go find him as soon as I finish here." Picking up a fork, she turned her attention with relish to her breakfast. *Maybe married life wasn't that bad after all.*

AGITATEDLY, Landon's forefinger tapped on the paper-strewn surface of his desk as his gaze flickered between his notes and the handwritten copies of Linear A that had been discovered in Crete. *There has to be something I'm missing.* He stared up at the wall in thought, catching sight of a framed photo of him at an archaeological dig. *That's where I should be now, not pretending to play happy couple.* Resentment left a bad taste in his mouth. *Grandfather is treating me like a pillock, and I'm letting it happen. Not that it's going particularly well.*

A gentle knock followed by a light fragrance announced Chora's arrival before she'd even glided into the room. It was the same perfume she'd been wearing the night before and the one he'd woken up to this morning. Landon watched her expression as she gazed around the room, eyes wide and ceaselessly moving as she took it all in. A thoughtful smile curved the line of her lips. "Winston said you would be in your study, but this is more like a library or something straight out of a regency romance." She gave an excited intake of breath. "You even have one of those ladders on the shelves."

"It's important that I can keep everything I need on hand." With a tip of his head, he motioned to his desk. "Cataloguing is one of the first things they taught us at university."

Chora came closer, staring down at the desk intently. "In your file, you mentioned you were an archaeologist. What are you researching?"

Landon wasn't sure when a woman he'd been dating had asked him about his work last. *But I'm not dating her. She's my wife,* he reminded himself. He looked at her, trying to gauge how serious she was in her question. Finding only lively curiosity, he decided to humor her.

"I specialize in the Minoan civilization and have spent a lot of my career working on digs and restoration in Crete—in particularly Knossos, Palekastro and Zakros."

Chora nodded thoughtfully. "Is this Minoan writing?" She indicated the source of his earlier frustrations.

"This is Linear A, and so far, has never been deciphered. Linear B, which is from the Mycenaean Greek age, shares some symbols, but it hasn't provided the clues that we need."

"Did they use some sort of paper like the Egyptians?"

"Papyrus? No, this was made using a stylus to cut lines into a tablet made of clay."

Her face brightened. "Oh, like cuneiform writing?"

Landon was startled that she knew what cuneiform was, but he shouldn't have been—he'd known she was intelligent. "Similar in that they both use a clay tablet, but cuneiform is stamped into it and this is cut."

"You said that Linear B shares some commonalities with Linear A. Have they been able to decipher anything?" Chora leaned forward, peering at the script like she could find a clue.

Landon found himself excitedly rummaging through his notes until he found the one he was after. "So far it has been divided into four main categories—numerals and metrical signs, phonetic signs, ligatures and composite signs, and ideograms. That's all we know. What they actually mean beyond that, we still don't know."

"That's so frustrating," blurted Chora, eyes wide in dismay.

"It is terribly inconvenient." Landon agreed. "Everything we know about Minoan society and life comes from the frescos and artwork we've uncovered. But to be able to actually translate text, the insight we would gain … well, one day."

"You need to promise me that as soon as they do, you tell me." Excitement shone in her eyes and polished her cheeks.

Landon marveled at the shared moment. No one outside of his colleagues had ever shown an interest in his career. One that he was passionate about. Inspiration hit him. "I think I have an idea for tonight's date, and this time I promise it won't matter what you wear."

∼

EACH BEAD WAS COOLLY smooth beneath Chora's fingertips as she rubbed them. "You look lovely tonight," Landon offered. *I thought I looked lovely last night, too.* She pushed the peevish thought away. "The style of necklace that you're wearing, the Squash Blossom, has imagery that can be found on petroglyphs that predate European contact in America."

Chora smoothed her turquoise necklace into place. "This was my grandmother's." She gave in to her curiosity. "What are petroglyphs?"

"Drawings that are carved into rock. It's believed that the Navajos were the first tribe to adopt the design before it spread to neighboring tribes."

"Yeah, and to every western fashion influencer after that."

"Regardless, it's a beautiful piece."

She swiveled in her seat to better look at Landon as he drove. "Are you going to tell me where we're going?"

"No."

"Mysterious."

"I'm not trying to be, but after the epic failure of last night, I don't want to get your hopes up." *Who knew all it took was some bonding over ancient history to break through that reserved exterior?*

Chora smiled into the darkness. Already tonight was going better than she'd anticipated. Intrigued, she looked at Landon as they pulled up in front of a grand building, large Grecian columns proudly standing guard. "Is that a museum?"

"Not just any museum. The British Museum. Now, if you'll kindly come with me, our evening awaits." He offered his black suit clad arm to her. Abuzz with what he could possibly have in store, she accepted. *Shouldn't the museum be closed?*

A security guard opened the door and an efficient young lady greeted them. "Lord Astley, I'm so glad we were able to help with your request. Your family has, after all, been quite generous to us, and we follow your Minoan work enthusiastically."

"Thank you for allowing access tonight, it is greatly appreciated." Landon followed the woman as they went through various rooms and halls. Chora could only gape at the treasures of antiquity that surrounded her. In the distance she could hear faint strains of classical music. A corridor and corner later, she found its source. A string quartet played discreetly in a corner, and a white cloth covered table set with glassware and a candle stood in the center of the room. Candlelight reflected off the glass cabinets, filled with priceless urns and ceramics.

"Where on earth are we?"

"I told you, the British Museum." Mischief twinkled in his eyes. *Or maybe it was just the reflected light she was mistaking it for.* "Oh, you mean here. This is where it all started for me. Well, not quite." He held her chair out for her expectantly and, bemused, she sat. "But suffice to say that this room right here had a monumental impact on me. This is the Minoan Room."

An attendant materialized at his side and poured some wine into his glass. "I hope you don't mind, but I've selected the wine to match our courses."

"Not at all. This right here—" She gestured at the string quartet, the room. Her mind was blown. "This is so outside of anything I've ever experienced that I think I'm just going to enjoy the ride."

"That's the spirit. Now the entrée—ah, here it is now."

Landon paused as bowls of pale brown liquid were placed in front of them. "It's wild mushroom and truffle cream soup. I hope that's suitable?"

"It sounds lovely." Chora sniffed delicately, the earthiness making her mouth water. "I have a slight addiction to truffle," she admitted. Her tastebuds erupted into ecstasy, an appreciative "oh" escaping her. "That's divine."

"I'm glad you enjoy it. It's one of my vices too." He made a show of closing his eyes as the spoon lingered on his lips.

Chora found herself unable to look away. A warmth filled her, and it wasn't solely from her meal. "I don't really know you that well, but this is the first time I've seen you be a bit more human. Actually, that's not right," she corrected herself. "Today in your study, that was the first time."

"We British tend to be a little more reserved by nature. We're not all therapy and talk show types like where you're from." A retort sprung to her lips, and before she could fling it at him, a flash of humor crossed his face. "Like how you're reacting now. That's not terribly British." His expression sobered. "The way I was raised, if you're a member of the aristocracy—especially an heir to a title—it's all about succeeding and being proper."

Chora's heart ached. *No wonder he appeared cold.* "It all seems really impersonal."

"My nanny was lovely. I cried when I had to leave her for boarding school."

"You had a nanny? So, your mom worked?"

"No, Mother didn't. But Nanny was there before my parents divorced. Once I left for Eton, my grandparents let her go."

"Why were your grandparents in charge of the nanny?"

"Because it was their house."

Chora really didn't know what to say, but didn't want to jeopardize it now that she'd finally gotten him talking. She cast her mind around for anything that would keep it going. "Is history a big thing in your family?'

"Not if you don't count lineage." He flashed that wry smile again as he took a sip of his wine. "I discovered my love of ancient history thanks to a teacher I had at Eton, and then Minoan culture thanks to a professor I had at Cambridge."

"That's very different to how I was raised." Chora couldn't think of two more different childhoods.

"Your file said your parents are still together."

"Yeah, I lived in Texas when I was little, and then Dad lost his job and we had to move to California and live with my grandparents. Actually, I guess that means we have something in common, after all."

"I'm going to assume you liked yours?" Landon leaned back as a waiter cleared his dish.

"My grandmother is actually the reason I love animals as much as I do." Grief still made her heart heavy when Chora thought about her grandmother no longer being with her.

"Then you were lucky. My grandparents aren't exactly the warm fuzzy type." Landon's brows were dark slashes as he stared moodily into his wineglass. "But it's reasonable to say they had just as lasting an effect on me as your grandmother did on you."

Watching the moment of sharedness disappear before her eyes, Chora began to fear the oft mentioned couple and what meeting them would bring.

CHAPTER 10

The room was the same as the previous morning when Chora woke up, but somehow the shadows seemed brighter, the air lighter. *What a revelation last night had been. Once the surface had been scratched, there had been a fascinating human being underneath.* Happily, she flew through her morning routine. *I hope Winston doesn't let me down on the breakfast front,* she thought as she made her way downstairs, the house no longer seeming as intimidatingly immense as it had before. The aroma of food hit her nose, and she had a vision of herself turning into a cartoon character and floating along in the air following it.

Smiling to herself at her frivolity, she entered the dining room and was pleasantly surprised to see Landon seated at the table. He folded his newspaper crisply and put down his teacup before rising and meeting her halfway. When he bent down and kissed her on the cheek, she was too startled to object.

"Good morning."

Flustered, Chora smoothed down her hair, feeling warmth flood her face. "Good morning."

Spying Winston, she felt silly. *It was all just an act for the butler's benefit.* Feeling more downcast than she should, she began to pile food on her plate. Today there seemed to be some sort of fish, and the eggs were scrambled. The rest remained the same. Carefully so as not to spill any of her food, she made her way over to the table.

"Coffee again, Lady Astley?" Winston solicitously inquired.

"Yes, please."

Landon waited while her cup was filled. "Did you enjoy yourself last night?'

"I did." She couldn't be sure, but if she didn't know better, she would think she saw a hint of smug delight cross his handsome features. "I don't think I'll ever forget a night like that."

"I didn't bore you then. It has been drawn to my attention at times that I have rather a tendency to let my passion for history overcome me."

"Not at all. In fact, quite the opposite. I like learning about new things, and it was really interesting."

He smiled at her, and she noticed that, somehow, his face seemed more relaxed. By no means was it fully animated, but it wasn't as stiffly formal as it had been. *Maybe we're making progress.* "You'll have to forgive me, but I will be on conference calls all day. But you should go into the city and do some shopping and see the sights. I'll give you my credit card in case there's anything you'd like to purchase."

Before Chora could answer, Winston reappeared. "Excuse me, Lord Astley, but Mr Orstwell is here to see you."

"There's no need to be so formal all the time, old chap. Laddy knows who I am." Chora stared at the man with wheat-colored hair who waltzed in, a certain openness to him. He stopped when he saw her. "Laddy, you sly dog. You never told me your new wife puts the very stars to shame."

He came over and kissed Chora's hand. Flustered for the second time over breakfast, she giggled and looked at Landon inquiringly.

"I didn't think you had to be told not to flirt with my wife." Landon's greeting contained a strong suggestion of reproach. *He almost sounded jealous.* "Chora, this is my friend, Freddy. Freddy, this is my wife, Chora."

"Enchante. Don't mind Laddy, he can be miserable first thing in the morning." Freddy began to help himself to some food.

"It's eight-thirty, old chum," Landon reminded his friend.

"That's what I said, first thing in the morning. Winston, do be a pal and get me a cup of coffee. Laddy's already being beastly to me." Chora giggled at the continued use of Landon's nickname. *I wonder if I could get away with calling him that, too.* "And what are you young lovers up to this morning?"

"Well, Landon is working, and I'm not really sure yet. It's just been suggested I go shopping." Chora took a bite of buttery toast.

"My sister loves shopping, and I'm pretty sure she has nothing planned except to wait around for her boyfriend," Freddy said, eagerly taking the coffee offered to him by Winston.

"So, you've had no luck with breaking that off?" Landon asked.

Freddy's expression spoke volumes. "He's no good. He treats her appallingly and yet still she remains with him. If I wasn't so bloody scared of him, I'd go give him a right thumping, but I'm terrified he'd top me. Bloody Russian mafia and all that."

"Well, maybe a shopping trip with Chora will prove to be the fix. She's quite forthright. Maybe she'll listen to her.'

Chora was a little surprised at the faith Landon had in her

to deal with someone she didn't know about something she knew nothing about. "Um, I guess. But do I really need to go shopping? I could just stay here and read a book or something."

"No, Laddy's right. She might listen to you. You know, woman to woman," Freddy pleaded.

"And you do need to go shopping. A weekend in the country will require some clothing that I'm not sure you've packed," Landon added.

Chora frowned at them ganging up on her, miffed that Landon was suggesting she didn't have anything suitable to wear. *Are we back to that again?* "What do you mean?"

"Do you have wellingtons?" asked Freddy. "That's usually a big one for the country."

"Um, no." *Who packed gumboots for an overseas trip anyway?*

"Formal attire for dinner?'

Chora wasn't sure if Landon was joking or not. "No. I didn't think we were meeting the Queen."

"You haven't met Laddy's grandparents then." Freddy fell silent after a quelling glare from Landon.

"Fine." She crossed her arms over her chest. "I know when I'm beaten. But I'm warning you, I won't feel bad about spending your money now." She poked her tongue out at both of them before calmly picking up her fork to resume eating. "So, what's your sister's name?"

"I'M ARABELLA, but you may call me Bella." Chora stared at the mesmerizing woman, an intimidating man standing discreetly behind her. "Oh, and you can just pretend Boris isn't here." The man mountain that was Boris didn't even twitch. It was beginning to feel like Chora had stepped into some sort of parallel universe. "Now, Freddy tells me you need some help with attire for this weekend."

"I didn't think I did, until Freddy and Landon decided I did," Chora tartly replied. It was embarrassing standing in front of this elegant, classy woman knowing that it had been decided that she was somehow lacking. *It's not like I don't know fashion. I come from LA, after all.*

Bella's red lips curved upwards as she gave a ladylike snort. "That's men for you. Always think they know what's best." She stepped forward, and with her expensive leather handbag hanging off one arm, linked her other with Chora. "The trick is to keep them thinking that while getting exactly what you want." Chora found herself being led up the pavement. "Now, it won't be a weekend in the country if you don't have a pair of Hunter Wellies and a stout, waxed jacket." Bella looked her over as they walked. "What evening dresses did you pack?"

"None." *How much clothing did she need for a simple weekend in the country? This was getting ridiculous!*

"Excellent."

Chora stared at Bella. "Why?"

"Because I love to shop and I'm very good at it, and Freddy gave me Laddy's credit card. I'm going to enjoy this."

There was something contagious about Bella's enthusiasm. Maybe this was going to be fun after all.

HEARING about the progress being made back at the dig site in Crete had made Landon keener than ever to return. *The sooner we can convince Grandfather, the sooner that can happen.* He felt a little guilty about wanting to ditch Chora so quickly. She was actually brilliant company now they'd found some sort of middle ground, and she'd been a real chum about it all. Even when his attitude had been less then sterling. Landon tried not to dwell on how he felt each time she walked into the room. It wasn't sensible to have that reaction to her when they both knew what the ending to their story would be.

He glanced at the clock. Chora should be coming home soon. *Maybe it hadn't been wise to let her go shopping with Bella. After all, Freddy said her boyfriend had connections with the Russian mafia...* Agitated at the thought, he stood, deciding that he would call Freddy and find out where his sister was. He'd only just emerged from his study when he almost bowled into a glowing Chora.

"Oh, I was just coming to see you."

Without conscious effort, he found himself returning her smile. It flickered slightly when he caught sight of Winston in the background unobtrusively dusting a balustrade. *That damn butler is always around.* Putting a large hand to her waist, he pulled Chora toward him and, before he could change his mind, pressed his lips to hers, more caressing than kissing. He released her and nonchalantly stepped back.

"I missed you, darling."

Chora's eyes were saucer wide, and she seemed a little short of breath. "I, ah, missed you too."

"I've arranged for us to catch up for drinks with my friends tonight. I thought it was high time I introduced you all. They're absolutely dying to meet you. I rather expect Freddy has already been gloating that he was the first to set eyes on you."

"Is there anything I need to know about dress code?" There was a saucy tilt to her chin that was rather fetching.

"Not this time. It's a members' club, but a little bit more progressive than the last one."

"I'll go freshen up then."

Landon watched her go. The kiss might have all been part

of the charade, but that didn't mean he hadn't enjoyed it—almost a little too much. *Maybe Winston needed to be around more.*

⌇

LANDON FOUND himself feeling quite smug as he watched his friends fall victim to Chora's charm, each vying for her attention. Alistair raised his glass to him. "You're a lucky bugger, aren't you?"

"I like to think that I was selective in who I chose for my wife."

"Pretend wife," Alistair corrected, a sly twinkle in his eye.

"Are we meant to be talking about this?" Stirling asked, making a show of looking around as if he expected a spy to leap out from behind the potted plant in the corner. "After all, we're in on the secret, but you never know who might be listening."

"I think we're fine," Freddy said, lounging in his chair. "Plus, we need to prepare this delicate young thing for the rigors of the weekend."

Chora laughed, an anxious shadow lurking in the depths of her eyes. "I'm sure it can't be that bad."

"Dear me, sometimes it's worse." Freddy dramatically clutched at his chest. Landon thought he was overplaying the part. "Everyone who's anyone will be there wanting to meet the woman who finally landed one of the most eligible lords in Britain. It's going to be a bloodbath, and that's assuming the old man is in a good mood. If he's not, it will be worse." Chora looked a little under the weather at the revelation.

"Stop filling her head with nonsense." Landon sent his friend a warning look. "There will, of course, be a reception. I believe Bella helped you select something suitable for that." He raised a brow in question.

"Yes, she did." Chora looked a little more reassured.

"I heard there are plans for a pheasant hunt," Stirling enthused. The man was a keen shooter.

"And taking the hounds hunting." Freddy rubbed his hands together.

Chora shook her head in a slow back and forth motion of denial. "Landon, you can't mean there will be hunting."

"It is rather a traditional country pastime." Landon wasn't sure he liked the way this was headed.

"You can't allow it to happen." Her eyes burned feverishly into his.

"You obviously haven't met the Duke." Alistair gave a short bark of laughter at the thought of telling Landon's grandfather what to do. "Never met a man who liked being told what to do less." *Especially by me.*

Chora's lips pressed tightly together, her nostrils flaring, but she held her tongue. The way she looked at him, Landon didn't think it was the end of the conversation. Not by a long shot.

CHAPTER 11

*P*ensively, Chora pushed the cooked mushrooms around her plate. This morning she couldn't even bear the thought of sausage. After last night's discussion, she'd decided to stick to a purely vegetarian plate to symbolize her protest over the proposed hunting on the weekend. Not that Landon had seemed to notice when he'd come down and greeted her with what was by now the familiar kiss on the top of the head if she was already seated or the much more intimate kiss if she entered after him. Of course, only if Winston was anywhere to be found.

"You made a good impression on the chaps last night." Landon folded his paper and set it to one side.

"They seem nice."

The bonds between them had been obvious. The teasing and stories of school and misadventures as they welcomed her to the fold, albeit only temporary, had been done with genuine warmth and affection. Watching Landon completely unguarded for the first time since Chora had met him had filled her with a surprising amount of happiness. That was until the hunting topic had raised its ugly head. What little remained of her appetite deserted her, and Chora pushed her plate away.

"Is there something wrong with your breakfast? I'm sure Winston can prepare something else."

Chora looked up to find herself on the receiving end of drawn eyebrows and inquiring eyes. "No, I don't want to bother him."

"He's a butler." One brow now shot up with an amused tilt to his lips. "His very job description is to be bothered by us."

"No, it's fine, thank you."

"Well, judging from the doldrums that you now seem to be in, it's a good idea I planned for us to attempt a bit of Zen before we enter the viper's nest this evening."

Chora's stomach dropped as fingers of dread danced up her spine. She wasn't sure if she was ready for this weekend —nor ever, given all she'd heard the previous evening. "What did you have planned?"

Landon pushed his chair back and rose, slowly making his way to her. "I was thinking maybe an Isopod session might be in order. I know I could do with one before we leave for the family country estate this afternoon." He held his hand out for her expectantly.

The warmth now chased the chill out of her bones. When he looked at her like that, well, it was easy to forget that this was all a charade. Her husband truly was a devastatingly handsome man. "I'm willing to try anything if it will help me get through meeting your family and not making a fool of myself."

"My darling Chora, I wish I could suit you up in armor to protect you from the barbs that will be flung carelessly at you. But I have complete faith that you will rise above it all." She let him draw her to her feet. "But for now, a float and a soak will have to suffice."

Side by side, they made their way past where Winston discreetly lingered, waiting to be summoned if required. *Remember, it's just a performance.* "You seem to have a lot of faith in this Isopod thing." It actually surprised her. It seemed a little airy-fairy for the likes of him.

He grimaced in good humor. "I know it's quite the done thing and I was hugely skeptical until my mother told me to try it one time when I was in a fit of pique with my work. There was something to floating in that warm water that opened up my mind and focused me. Not to mention it did wonders for my aching body from the dig. Since then, I try to have a session regularly." He opened the passenger door for her. Chora was surprised to find they had already made their way to his car. "I'm actually really looking forward to hearing about what your experience is like."

Somehow in the last few days a comradery had grown between them. It surprised Chora that she was beginning to look at this complicated man as her friend. As he began to shed his formality around her, she began to enjoy the glimpses of warm wit and intelligence that he shared with her. She settled back into her seat. *I wonder what clarity I will achieve from this Isopuddle contraption.*

DELICIOUS WARMTH WRAPPED AROUND HER. In the darkness, it was impossible to tell where her body ended and the water began. Almost as if the water she floated weightless in was somehow one and the same as her. Dreamlike, her thoughts began to flow. Landon, coldly practical, outlining his proposal in the bright Californian sun, crisply handsome despite the heat. Landon emerging from his sleek sportscar onto the wetly gleaming tarmac as she set foot in England. The sense of relief at seeing him there waiting for her.

Feeling small and alone as she followed his retreating back, fleeing from the mocking glances of the faceless diners at the club. Passion sparking from him as he talked about the Minoans, all remoteness disappearing and somehow drawing her in closer to him. Visions of women dancing with snakes and speaking ancient languages mingling with him. Laughing friends offering hands to her and pulling her close. A fox and a pheasant hiding under the table.

Dim colored lights and muted music returned her to once again floating in a capsule. Somehow, she felt lighter, freer, connected. *Maybe Landon was on to something.* Stepping from the water, she found the weight of her own body jarring, as if gravity had somehow become stronger. Her mind, however, seemed to still float along. *Hopefully it stays for the weekend. Heaven knows I need it.* Turning the shower on to wash away the salt that was already crystallizing on her skin, she closed her eyes. *Time to leave and play the role of a lifetime. Time to be Landon's wife.*

THE LONG DRIVE over the stone bridge spanning the brook had the gardens and woodlands welcoming them while the country house rising in the distance stood as if looking down on them in judgment. Beside him, Chora gave a little gasp each time she spied something new. *It was to be expected.* Landon considered the spectacle from her point of view. The gardens had been a welcome escape from the house when he'd been younger, the gardeners often taking pity on him and letting him help with the digging and planting. *Maybe that's why I became an archaeologist. I could very well have ended up a gardener.* Landon mulled that thought over. *Would it really have been that terrible working in the soil and watching life replenish itself?*

"Landon, this place is amazing." Awe tinged Chora's slightly breathless voice.

"Would you like the brief history of it before we meet my grandparents? I can drive slower just so we have enough time." *Or delay the inevitable.*

"I'd love that." She turned brightly shining eyes to him, and he found himself smiling back at her excitement.

"What you see around you is over two thousand acres of garden, designed back in the day by the same chap who did the Palace of Westminster. You can't see all of it, obviously, but take my word for it. There is a maze, formal gardens, stables, kitchen gardens, water terraces, private Italian gardens, secret gardens and rose gardens."

Chora blinked at him. "That's a lot of gardens."

"I guess it gave all the previous dukes and duchesses something to do when they came to the country."

"Has it been in your family long?"

"It's been the family seat of the Dukes of Beaumond for the last two hundred and fifty years which, considering it took over one hundred years to build the pile of rocks, is a good thing." Landon might not hold his grandfather and late father in the highest esteem, but there was something about knowing the long line of men and women who came before him that did on occasion fill him with pride. "Now, the building you see ahead, the one to the left?"

"Yes?" Chora leaned forward, peering through the windscreen. "Is that where guests stay?"

"That's the stables."

Her mouth opened wide. "No way!"

"Way. The building beside it is the main house. It has two hundred rooms and over one thousand windows. A funny side note, you used to have to pay taxes on the number of windows in your house."

"Landon, that isn't a house, that's a palace." Chora was beginning to look a little wild around her eyes.

"Well, it was pressed into service during World War II as a hospital."

Chora appeared to be doing her level best to disappear into the upholstery of her seat as they pulled in front of the grand stone staircases that led up to the house. "I think I feel sick."

"My grandparents tend to have that effect on people." Landon could see the butler making his way down to meet them. He took Chora's hand in his, driven by an unexpected need to comfort her. "I will be with you every step of the way, and when I can't, my friends will arrive tomorrow and will gallantly fill the void. After this weekend, we're a step closer to our goal." *And once again having an ocean between us.* Unsettled by his thought, he cleared his throat. "Let's go meet the Duke and Duchess of Beaumond."

Opening the door, he made his way around to Chora, the butler, Benson, hovering, ready to swoop on their luggage. "Lord Astley, Lady Astley," he intoned with a nod of his head.

"Benson, I trust you have been in good health." Landon had a soft spot for the old butler—he'd been in the house since he was a baby. A gruff, firm, but always reliable presence to his childhood. Even if his first loyalty was to the Duke.

"Exceedingly so."

"Excellent. And my grandparents?"

"They are waiting for you in the Duke's library."

Of course. It might have sounded like a casual location to meet his new wife, but Landon knew it was anything but. The library was the very seat of Grandfather's power in the house. "Chora, my darling." He held out his arm.

"Yes, dear." He blinked at the brilliance of her adoring smile as she linked her arm with his.

He led her up the stone staircase and through the grand front entrance. From time to time as they made their way, he felt her footsteps falter as she took it all in. The painted hallways filled with their priceless, beautiful artworks in particular seemed to stun her. He even thought he heard a mumbled "Glorious," under her breath as they passed beneath the gleaming white rotunda until, at last, the heavy wooden door of the library waited before them.

"Ready?"

"As I'll ever be." Her hand trembled ever so slightly on his arm before she took a deep breath and, chin raised, gave him a smile of pure determination.

"That's the spirit." Pushing the door open, he led them in.

The library was exactly as it always had been. That was the thing with the aristocracy—they didn't really embrace change. From the antique rugs on the floor to the heavy wood paneling, the shelves groaning under first edition manuscripts and the hounds sleeping in front of the hearth.

"So, you've finally graced us with your presence." The grizzled man seated behind his expansive desk growled, disapproval stamped over his wrinkled countenance.

"Simon," protested the silver-haired woman seated on the settee beside him. His grandmother rose and made her way over. "Landon, I've missed you, and this is your beautiful bride. I'm pleased to meet you at last."

"I've missed you too, Grandmother, and let me introduce you to Chora. Chora, this is my grandmother, Esme, and grandfather, the Duke of Beaumond." He could feel his wife's questioning gaze at the formality he gave the old man.

"I hear you were thrown out of a members only club." Grandfather's mouth had turned mean, bushy brows slanted downwards like hairy caterpillars. *Trust the news to have already reached his ears.* "You need to make sure your wife knows how to behave in a way that befits her new station."

"It was just a terrible misunderstanding." Chora's hand flew delicately to her chest. "One that I won't make again, I can promise you." She gazed up at him with wide-eyed devotion. A funny feeling stole over him at the look. "Landon has been marvelous in helping me find my feet here in England."

He lifted her hand to his lips and kissed it delicately. The disgusted look on his grandfather's face was only half the reason he chose to do so. "You will have to forgive my lapse in judgment, but we are still very much in the honeymoon stage. After spending time in LA, I'd forgotten how stuffy things can be here."

Grandmother looked between the locked gazes of the two men in the room, quickly inserting herself between them. "I've arranged for Cook to prepare some trays. I thought perhaps you might wish to dine in your rooms tonight. After all, Chora, you must be feeling a bit tired from all your traveling." Landon could happily kiss the old woman. She'd always played peacemaker. "After a good night's sleep, you'll be quite refreshed for the festivities of the weekend."

"Thank you, that's very kind of you," Chora said.

"Well, if that's all arranged, Chora and I will retire to our rooms." Landon didn't wait for his grandfather's acknowledgement before sweeping from the room, his wife beside him.

"I think we did well," Chora whispered as he marched along.

"Don't congratulate yourself too soon." He took a right down another hallway. "That was just a warning shot. He's testing us." Up another flight of stairs.

"Your grandmother seems nice."

Ah, at last. Landon opened up the door to their rooms, exhaling as he closed the door behind them. "Grandmother is nice, but she is also very aware of social status and etiquette." He watched as Chora looked around the room. *This all must seem like a different planet to her. Most of the time now it does to me, and I was born to it.* "Tomorrow, the guests will start arriving. People will be watching us. What do you know about rank?"

"Like in the military?" Chora looked back at him from where she was at the window, peering at the view before her.

"No, like in aristocracy."

"The Queen is important?" she offered hesitantly.

"You're right. At the top is the King and currently the Queen. Below them are dukes and duchesses—my grandparents, for example. Then I'm a marquess and you are a marchioness, earls and countesses—my uncle is an earl, which he inherited through my grandmother's family. Then viscounts and viscountess and below them are the barons and baronesses. My grandparents should be referred to as Your Grace, but they will be the only ones of that rank present this weekend. Everyone else you can refer to as Lord or Lady, unless they have no title. Try to remember when you have precedence, especially at dinner."

"Except for you, your grandparents are the first members of aristocracy I've ever met. It's actually a little daunting." Chora made her way over to the bed and sat down.

"That's actually not true. Freddy is a Baron, and Stirling is due to be a Viscount when his father passes."

She stared back at him. "Really? They seemed almost normal."

He gave a bark of laughter. "I can't wait to tell them that."

"Well, you know what I mean. What about Alistair?"

Landon laughed harder. "There's nothing normal about Alistair. He's a bloody Aussie convict!"

"You know what I mean. Is he something as well?"

"He doesn't have to be. His parents own cattle stations— one of which is almost bigger than Belgium. I believe it's roughly twenty-four thousand square kilometers, or just over six million acres. And that's just one of them. They also happen to own several iron ore mines. Alistair doesn't need a title, trust me. He's painful enough without one." Landon gathered some pillows from the bed and retrieved a blanket from a wardrobe in preparation for creating a nest on the floor. The polished floorboards didn't look particularly inviting.

Chora leaned back on her arms, sharing a pained look with him. "Don't take this as anything more than what I'm offering, but it doesn't look like it would be very comfortable sleeping on the floor. At least at your place you had the sofa. You can sleep on the bed, like, above the covers with a blanket over you, and I'll sleep under the covers. Just for while we're here."

"Well, that's right neighborly of you," he said in his best Texan twang. He gathered up his nest materials and relocated them to one side of the bed. "Actually, you're the best wife I've ever had."

Chora laughed merrily—the sound, he was sure, would lift the lowest of spirits. "I hope so."

Later after they'd eaten their fill from their dinner trays and had both retired for the night, Landon began to wonder at the wisdom of sleeping on top of the bed. Each time she moved, he was intensely aware that she was a mere arm's length away from him. He did, however, find himself smiling at the little puffs of breath she gave in her sleep like a little kitten. A little kitten who was his wife. Sighing, he rolled onto his side and prayed for sleep.

CHAPTER 12

A breakfast tray had thankfully been delivered to the room that morning, sparing Chora the experience of sitting down to breakfast with the Duke and Duchess. She could've hugged Landon when he'd suggested he would give her a tour of the grounds.

Now strolling beside him, it felt like every turn in the gravel path led to another marvel. "I can't imagine what it was like growing up here." She gazed out over a water terrace, the cascades ending in a deep square pool filled with frolicking nymphs and chubby cherubs.

"I learned very early not to touch anything in the house. You have no idea how many times I was told that the art collection was not to be played with. It did take over four centuries to acquire well before they acquired this old pile, so Nanny might've had a point. Then there was the time I hid in the stateroom and fell asleep. Apparently, that caused quite the ruckus."

"I can imagine, but what's a stateroom?" Chora loved getting these little glimpses into Landon's childhood.

"Back when it was traditional for the King and Queen to

tour the countryside each year, it was expected that the estates had rooms that were suitable for their use if they came. The rooms are richly decorated and appointed and no one else uses them."

"Did the King and Queen come often?"

"Only once in the history of the Dukedom."

Chora stared at him. "Are you telling me that in the last couple of centuries there's a room in that building that has only been used once?"

Her reaction seemed to amuse him, one side of his mouth twitching. "Well, except for when I fell asleep on one of the beds. And I suppose you could consider the cleaning and changing of linen as it being used."

"That's so next level," she spluttered.

"Well, that's what happens when you live in a building with over two hundred rooms." A mischievousness flickered across his face as he glanced at her, sending a flutter of breathlessness through her. "Would you like to explore the maze?"

"Of course. I'd almost forgotten you have a maze."

"Imagine the embarrassment if we didn't. We wouldn't be able to show our faces in society." He reached down and took hold of her hand. Chora was intensely aware of his touch. Here in the garden, it seemed somehow more intimate. "It's best you stay close. I wouldn't want you to get lost. It's not quite a labyrinth and there's definitely no Minotaur, but I'd hate to have to explain how I lost my wife—and when I'd only just found her, too."

Chora giggled. "You are in the silliest mood I've seen you in since I've known you."

Landon's expression turned serious, not quite hiding the mirth lurking in his eyes. "You'll have to forgive me. It must be all the fresh air."

Playfully, she swatted at his arm. "Well, don't let it become a habit. I might get used to it otherwise."

Winking at her, Landon led her around the first corner of the maze. "We can't have that happening."

Before she knew it, time had passed in fits of laughter and teasing. When they'd reached the center of the maze, the private garden and sundial had been gorgeous. Standing there in bright sunshine, she'd found herself wondering if this was the same man she'd first met. Somehow over the last couple of days, it seemed like he'd always been there. Chora mused over the realization as they made their way back into the bowels of the maze again. Rounding a corner, she found to her disappointment that they'd now returned to the outside world.

"Is it my imagination, or did that take less time than going in?"

"It might have been the expert guidance you received from yours truly." Landon gave her a courtly bow. "Now, if my eyes don't deceive me, it looks like the guests are arriving." He held his hand out to her. "Shall we?"

Chora looked down at it. There was a strength to his hands that was at odds with his sophisticated air. The man was full of paradoxes. Taking it, she smiled at him. "Let's do this."

CHORA CLUNG TO HIS ARM, casting him an infatuated glance before returning to whatever it was the Honorable Milly Cartwright was saying to her. Landon had long extracted himself from that conversation after exchanging polite niceties and contented himself with sending mutinous looks to his blackguard friends who'd failed to come and rescue him.

"It was such a shock to hear that Landon had married," Miss Cartwright continued to Chora. "I mean, we all thought he'd decided to commit himself to his work like some pagan. And then to find out it was to an American and that you don't even come from family money." Her face took on a scandalized expression.

Landon had finally had enough. If his friends couldn't be counted on, then he was going to have to do it himself. "I think you will find it was because the ladies I was being introduced to all seemed a little lackluster, but Chora here"—he patted his wife's hand affectionately—"is pure light. Now, if you'll excuse us, I think it's time we mingle. Can't have you monopolizing us now, can we?" Ignoring Miss Cartwright's indignant gasp, he firmly strode away, Chora in tow.

"Wasn't that a little rude?" his wife murmured, smiling at several people as they passed.

"Did you want to hear more?" He pretended to slow down as if to return her. "I can take you back."

"Don't you dare."

His freedom was short-lived. "Actually, I'm rather beginning to regret having made our escape. Grandfather is waving us over, and to add to the joy, my uncle is with him." Landon's blood pressure was already increasing. *It had been naïve of me to think he would miss this opportunity.*

"Should I get a drink before we head over?" Chora discreetly cast a look in his family's direction.

"It'll take something stronger than that to not feel like you've been lobotomized before it's over." Landon scowled.

"Let's get it over with." She assumed an expression of complete unconcern. *At least, I think she's assuming it.*

Landon fought to assume his normal bored visage, all while battling the urge to wipe the smug look off his uncle's face. *He shouldn't be standing there smirking. He should be sulk-*

ing. After all, I've just secured my inheritance. "Grandfather, Uncle." He nodded.

"Landon, I see you've managed to get yourself a bride—and in the nick of time, too." Uncle raised his glass and peered at Chora, hard skepticism etched on his face. "Awfully convenient."

The thud of his blood pounding in his ears was deafening. "When you know, you know."

"Really?" The other man still looked at his wife as one would a horse they wished to buy.

Unbidden, Landon found his fist clenching. "Really."

"I expect you to join us for the pheasant hunt this afternoon." Grandfather's tone brooked no argument. Apparently Chora didn't pick up on it.

"Hunting? I can't do that." Her brows folded in over horrified eyes. Nose crinkled, she turned pleading eyes to Landon. "This is a joke, right?"

"My dear girl, what do you think we do in the country? Play charades?" Uncle sneered in derision.

"Mind your tone," Landon warned, stepping closer to Chora. "My wife is a passionate animal advocate. She fronts a charity called Animals Are Forever, and as you can guess, the idea of hunting is somewhat distasteful to her."

"I think your wife would be surprised at how little I care what she thinks." Uncle's mocking chuckle turned Landon's blood boiling. "You need to train her better."

"Train? I'm not some horse." Chora's nostrils flared.

"If you were, I'd expect my nephew to have paid more attention to your bloodlines." She drew in a sharp breath at the insult. Landon had had enough. He took a threatening step forward.

Grandfather raised his hand for peace. "Apologize, Charles."

A smarmy look of pure insincerity only served to intensify Landon's anger. "I'm sorry if you took offense, it was only a little fun."

Chora's lips pressed together in a white, bloodless line, and a shimmer was in her eyes. "I think we have different ideas of fun. If you'll excuse me, I find that I suddenly have a headache." With a gloriously defiant toss of her head, she spun on her heels and strode away.

Landon could only satisfy himself with a final glare of promise before following in her wake and out of the room. "I'm sorry, there's no excuse for his behavior."

"That is the most odious man I've ever met." Her eyes were flinty as she narrowed them. "And yes, I just said odious. Is there really going to be a pheasant hunt?"

"It appears so. We did discuss it at dinner the other night"

She rounded on him. "But did you know I would be forced to attend?"

"I didn't. I should've assumed there would be one, however, and I'm sorry I didn't think to tell Grandfather in advance that it wouldn't be suitable for you to attend." Landon felt like a cur. *Why didn't I think of it?*

She stepped forward and gripped his arm tightly, her nails biting through his sleeves. "You've got to stop it."

"You have met my grandfather, right? Does he seem like he's stoppable?"

"This weekend is about us, to celebrate our marriage. Surely he can be reasoned with."

The way she looked at him, pleading … well, he was ready to go out to the painted great hall and strap on the suit of armor on display there. "I can try."

Landon staggered under her weight as she unexpectedly threw herself at him, wrapping her arms fiercely around him. "Thank you."

"I wouldn't thank me yet. I haven't changed his mind, and I honestly doubt I will."

Chora's eyes glowed as she beamed at him. "But you'll try, and I have complete faith in you."

Great, she isn't going to be disappointed at all. "Let me wait until he goes to his library. He might be a little more approachable there."

"That sounds like a good plan. Do you think you can make my excuses? I really do have a headache beginning."

"Of course. Is there anything I can do?"

"Talk to your grandfather."

He smiled at her persistence. "Yes, Lady Astley. I'll have a tray of food sent up."

"And come and tell me everything when you're finished."

He touched his fingers to his forehead in a gallant salute. "As my lady commands." If only he felt as confident as he sounded.

AFTER WHAT SEEMED like hours making polite chitchat and apologies for Chora having retired early, Landon finally spotted his opportunity when his grandfather departed to his library to have a sherry with some of his cronies. Seeing his uncle hadn't followed, Landon wasn't about to squander and followed after them with haste.

Grandfather arched an eyebrow at him imperiously when he entered his private sanctuary. "Well, don't stand there like a stuffed goose. What do you want?" He always had the knack to make him feel like a gauche child.

Squaring his shoulders, he sought to find just the right tone with which to address the old man. Grandfather didn't like weakness, but neither did he relish not being in control. "Chora is quite distressed at the prospect of the shoot. Is there any chance of getting it canceled?"

"Are you daft? The guns are being prepared as we speak.

What's wrong with the girl?" He looked around at his chortling friends. "She needs a little more backbone."

"My wife's backbone is fine. But she is passionate about animal welfare and the thought of the shoot has caused her to retire early. Would you consider canceling it in the nature of a wedding gift?"

"Next you'll be asking me to cancel the fox hunt tomorrow." More spluttering laughter.

Landon tried to bottle the need to lash out. Only a cool head would prevail here. "Imagine how generous that gift would be. Everyone knows how much you enjoy your traditions. To welcome a new bride into the family and showing support by canceling the shoot and changing tomorrow's hunt to a drag hunt. Well, I can't think of a more magnanimous gesture."

He waited, his grandfather's expression indecipherable. "I guess I can grant this as a wedding gift. But boy, you might consider not being under your wife's thumb, especially this early in the marriage. It's not a good precedent to set."

Landon nodded, not trusting himself to do more than smile for a moment. "Chora will be extremely grateful at your generous gesture."

"Then run off and tell her. We can't have her sulking in her room for the entire weekend. It's embarrassing."

And that's what we worry about in this family. Appearances and what other people think. With studied calm, Landon took his leave and made his way back to their rooms to find Chora agitatedly pacing in front of the fireplace. "You'll wear a track in the rug. It's pretty old."

Guiltily, she glanced down as she came to a halt. "So, this rug is more important than the birds?"

"I didn't say that."

She lifted her chin. Landon was taken aback by the tears

simmering in them. "I hate the thought of what's about to happen. He didn't change his mind, did he?"

"Such little faith in your husband."

Chora's eyes grew wide. "Are you saying—"

"That not only did I get him to cancel the shoot this afternoon, but also to change the hunt tomorrow to a drag hunt." He made a show of blowing on his fingers and buffing his nails on his shirt front. "I am a man of many talents, it transpires."

For the second time that evening, she threw herself into his arms. "Oh, Landon. Thank you, thank you, thank you." Chora sniffled between each one. *It really does mean so much to her.*

"Now, you can ride, can't you?"

Affronted, she pulled back. "Of course I can. I might have spent more time in California than in Texas, but I'm still a cowgirl at heart."

"Well, then did Bella help you purchase any riding clothes perchance?"

"Um, not that I remember."

"It's not her fault. I didn't think to mention that you might need some. I'll go ask Grandmother if there are some you can borrow."

"It's actually quite an exciting prospect." Chora plopped down on the bed.

"Me going to ask Grandmother for riding clothes?" Landon couldn't resist teasing her, although he wasn't entirely sure what she was excited about. All he knew was that the flush of color to her tanned cheeks was more appealing than all the coy smiles he'd been on the receiving end of that day.

"No, silly. The chance to ride through the English countryside. And the fact I haven't been on a horse for a few years."

Landon grinned at her. "I don't think you entirely comprehend what it's going to be like tomorrow. It's not going to be a leisurely ride."

She folded her arms across her chest as she glared a challenge at him. "Are you saying you don't think I can do it?"

"I don't have a death wish," he threw back at her lightly. "If there's one thing I've learned since I met you, it's that I would never assume to tell you anything." Landon winked at her, enjoying the playful narrowing of her eyes. She really was fun to tease. "Now, I best go find some riding clothes for you." Whistling softly, he left her. Thoughts of her in riding breeches was quite appealing.

Somewhere in the darkness beside her, Chora could feel the slow movements of Landon sleeping. She wasn't used to sharing a bed, even if that other person was sleeping on top of the covers. Heck, she wasn't even sure if she'd picked the side she preferred. *Such a rookie.* She picked up her phone to check in on her emails. Soon enough, Landon would be awake, and then it would be time to take turns showering and heading down for breakfast. She felt jittery at the planned hunt today—it was all completely foreign to her. Which had become abundantly clear when Landon had returned with the clothing he'd managed to borrow for her. One thing was for sure—she wasn't riding in Texas!

The jarring ring of her phone had her almost leaping out of her skin. Quickly, she silenced it before it could wake Landon and made her way to the bathroom. Once the door was secured behind her, she answered. "Hello, Misty."

"Don't 'hello, Misty' me," her friend replied tartly. "Is it true?"

"That you're Misty?"

"Don't play coy with me. I just got off the phone with someone at your charity, Crystal? Charisma?"

Chora should've known who would spill the beans first. "Christina?"

"Could be, and she told me that you're married, but I told her there's no way that would happen. Is there something you want to tell me?"

"Surprise?" She could almost picture Misty's face turning an extraordinary shade of red on the other end. Misty hated being out of the loop. "Look, it all happened in a bit of a rush."

"Are you pregnant?"

"No." Chora spluttered at the biological impossibility of that happening.

"I didn't even know you were seeing anyone."

Somehow this had seemed easier when she'd told Christina. She didn't want to lie to her friend, but at the same time, she wasn't sure she could tell her all of the truth as well. "It was an arranged date, and his name is Landon. Well, Lord Astley. He's a marquess, as it turns out."

"What I don't understand is how you went from an arranged date to marrying a marquess?'

Wasn't that the loaded question? "Um, well. It's in the nature of a business arrangement. He needed to get married, and as it turned out, so did I."

Silence, stark in its emptiness. "Are you in trouble? Is he blackmailing you in some way? If he is, I know people who can make him disappear." The deadly intensity in Misty's voice was vaguely scary. It also made her love her friend even more.

"No, it's not like that. I'm fine. He's actually really nice." *And handsome and kind. Not to mention funny and smart.*

"I don't think just being nice is reason enough to marry someone."

"It's a marriage in name only." It was no use. Misty was never going to drop it. It was time she came clean. "I made an error in judgment which resulted in all the money for the charity being embezzled." Shame made her throat tighten as she fought against mortifying tears. "And this marriage will fix it all."

"Oh, Chora. Why didn't you come to me? You know I would've been able to help."

She sniffed, blinking hard. "Because I was so embarrassed by what had happened after all the money you helped raise, and then Landon came along and offered me money to marry him in name only for a year. And that's how I became Lady Astley." Chora tried to finish lightheartedly. "I know what I'm doing."

"Well, it's done now, isn't it? But I still wished you'd come to me rather than doing it. It just seems a little drastic. What's he really like?"

"Well, he's nice."

"You said that before."

"He's interesting and rather smart. Landon's an archaeologist, actually." *Who's caring and loyal and funny.* Chora blinked, pulling her thoughts together. She was beginning to think like a silly schoolgirl with a crush. "He's terribly British."

"Look, I need to go. I promised Logan I would be in bed an hour ago, but I had to wait until I thought you would be awake enough to answer the phone. I'm still put out with you."

"I know."

"But I can respect that you're doing what you think needs to be done. That doesn't mean that I'm not going to get him checked out."

Chora smiled. "I wouldn't expect anything else."

"Next time, you come to me, agree?"

"Totally." *There wasn't going to be a next time.*

"When do you think you'll be back home?"

"Another week."

After exchanging goodbyes, Chora sat on the edge of the bath, staring at her phone. It seemed like a lifetime ago that she'd decided to marry Landon, and now he just seemed like a normal part of her life. Sighing, she turned on the shower. She might as well start getting ready for the bloodbath that was bound to be breakfast.

It turned out that everyone was so focused and giddy with excitement for the hunt that very little attention had been paid to her. Landon's friends had inquired after her health. Freddy, with a cheeky wink, had suggested loudly that it was due to the rigors of being newlyweds. Chora had almost choked on her coffee, and Alistair seated beside her had helpfully thumped her on the back. Landon's grandmother had solicitously offered the cook to make her something more fortifying, and Stirling had sniggered under his breath, earning him a kick under the table from Landon. It felt like Chora was surrounded by children.

Now standing in front of the mirror, she tried to contain her tresses in the hairnet Landon had given her, tucked into the velvet covered helmet. The navy color perfectly matched her jacket. "Can I help you with that?" Sighing, she handed the offending item to him. With quick deft movements, he secured it around her bun, fitting pins snuggly in place. "There, that should do it."

Chora gazed at him in the reflection. "You seem to have a bit of practice."

"It looks that way," he replied affably, not giving anything away.

She wondered which of the ladies present this weekend had been in need of his services before. "How do I look?" Chora gave a slow spin. Even though every inch of her skin was covered from the snowy white stock at her throat to her fawn breeches and black top boots, she somehow felt overexposed. *What's wrong with jeans?*

The slow travel of his appraising gaze brought a flush of warmth spreading from her belly to her cheeks. When he finally returned to her eyes, the glow of approval she saw there was gratifying, even if her mouth was too dry to swallow. "I don't think I've seen you wear anything that you didn't look good in, but this might be my favorite so far." *Is he flirting with me?* He looked rather handsome himself in his breeches and boots. Chora gazed at him, lips pursed as she considered what he'd look like in low slung jeans—shirt off, of course. He'd always been covered around her, but didn't seem like he carried any extra pounds. "Well then?" She blinked, finding him staring at her in exasperation as he held his hand out.

"Um, what?"

"Are you ready to go down to the stables and meet your horse?" From his tone, it was clear he'd already said it more than once.

"Yes. Do you know who I'll be riding?"

"I haven't been told yet, but don't worry. I know them all, so I'll be able to tell you if your mount is suitable or not." The heels of their boots click-clacked as they made their way through the painted hallway, other guests smiling or nodding as they passed.

Landon's friends fell into step beside them. "Are you excited?" Alistair asked. "I think except for tea and biscuits this is perhaps one of the most English things you can do. At least if you're a bit toffy."

"Toffy?" protested Freddy. "I resemble that remark and rather enjoy my biscuits."

Landon patted him on the belly. "It looks like it, too."

"The stress of dealing with Bella." Freddy affected a

wounded expression. "I didn't think you the sort to kick a man when he's low."

"Honestly, Freddy, I've seen better acting at the last auditions I had to sit through, and it was for child actors." Stirling nudged his sulky friend. "Now, back to our blushing bride. I say, you do look smashing."

Chora laughed self-consciously. "At least I'll look the part if I fall off."

Landon frowned at her. "I thought you said you could ride."

"I can, but I've never ridden in clothes like this or in anything but a western saddle."

"I feel your pain." Alistair gave a hearty laugh. "The first time I saw the tiny bloody thing they call saddles over here, I asked where the rest of it was. Give me a stock saddle any day. A man needs something to grip on to."

"I believe it comes down to being an expert horseman and not needing that something," Freddy said piously.

Chora was surprised to find that they were already at their destination. Horses, hounds and people were milling around. Landon quickly spoke to someone, and two horses were led out of their stables already tacked up—a non-script brown horse with a plain workmanlike head standing at well over seventeen hands, and a slightly smaller glistening bay with a white star.

"This," Landon said, taking the reins of the bay and walking her over to Chora, "is Gloria and she will be your horse for today. She's quite a nice mare and very experienced. She'll look after you." He checked the girth before fiddling with her stirrups. "I believe they should be a good length. Just remember, they will feel a bit short, but since we'll be going over jumps, that's how they should be." Chora stared dubiously at where they dangled at her shoulder height. *How on earth am I meant to get on there?* "Can I give milady a leg up?" Landon said in his best Artful Dodger impersonation.

"Yes." Now that the moment was here, her excitement had been replaced with a healthy dose of nerves. Once she was safely seated in the saddle, the pliable leather reins in her hands, she began to feel a little better. Gloria calmly walked around in a small circle when she asked her to while she waited for Landon to mount. Her horse didn't seem too worried about the commotion in the yard.

"Some port, my lady?" A man appeared at her side and handed her a small glass. Quickly, she drank it down, praying it would give her courage on the hunt.

"Well, it's all going to be terribly dull now," the uncle's voice drifted over to her. "Fancy making us all suffer just because she's giddy over a bit of blood." The group surrounding him laughed. *I'll show him a bit blood.*

She set her path for the odious man when Landon materialized at her side, looking down at her from his horse's superior height. "Zeus is feeling a bit fresh this morning," he said as the horse jogged, tossing his head.

Chora's reply was drowned out as the Field Master stepped forward and began to address them. She tried to remember everything he said, adding to her nerves. Inside her gloves, she could feel her palms sweating. The harsh cry of "Hounds, please!" and a horn being blown set forth the dogs spilling between the horses' legs, setting Zeus to dancing even more. Gloria, for her part, gave a loud snort, but otherwise remained calm.

"Are you ready?" There was a fierce gleam in Landon's eyes as he gathered up his reins.

"As I'll ever be."

The hounds raced away, noses to the ground, and then, as one great tide of horseflesh, the riders followed. Not in the mad gallop as Chora had anticipated, but a brisk trot. With each post she did, it felt like she was standing out of the saddle too much—thanks to her short stirrups—adding to her sensation of being perched precariously. Down the gravel path they trooped until they reached an open field and then they were off. Gloria, much more in charge than Chora, settled in a gallop that ate up the ground. Chora leaned forward and allowed her horse to stretch her neck, the cool air making her nose run. Knowing no animal would be slaughtered at the end of the exhilarating ride, she allowed a thrilling aliveness to zing through her. Beside her, Zeus loomed large, his rider urging him on to take the lead. *Not on my watch!* Nudging the mare with her legs, Chora willed her forward, a wildly primal need to match him. From the corner of her eye, she could see the fierce gleam in his. Stride for stride, they flew over fields and fences, hedges and ditches, and never once did one draw ahead of the other. Maybe she'd met her match.

THERE WAS something about the after-hunt tea. Landon's body felt deliciously empty and drained. Seeing Chora on that horse riding like a Valkyrie had made his blood course. He looked around for her. She'd excused herself earlier and hadn't reappeared.

"Isn't that right, Laddy?' Freddy asked.

Landon returned his attention to his friends and found them all staring back at him. "What?"

"He's bloody off with the fairies," Alistair sniggered. "Or should I say the sheilas—or just one in particular?"

"She's not a sheila, she's my wife." Landon's friends exploded into laughter. "I don't see what's so terribly funny."

Stirling dramatically looked around before leaning into

the center of the group and, in his best stage whisper, said, "I thought this was a business arrangement."

Landon gave him a cool look. "It is."

"You seem awfully attached to her," Freddy said, looking casually around as he sipped his brandy.

"She's a nice person." *I need to get new friends.*

"It seems like it's a little more than her being a bloody nice person." Alistair looked at Freddy and Stirling for support. The friends were quick to nod in agreement. "I mean, I think she's a nice person too," he quickly added.

"I think you're reading a little too much into it. Have you impertinent lot considered that if Chora and I can fool you, then everyone else is a piece of cake?"

"Touché, old chap." Freddy raised his glass in mock salute. "Are you going to go look?"

"Look for what?"

"For whom, dear boy." Freddy smiled smugly at Landon. "For your nice Chora."

Scowling at them, Landon retreated, muttering darkly ominous threats to their continued health as he walked off in the direction he'd last seen Chora depart. Just outside, he found her back against the wall as several women crowded around, peppering her with questions. Spying him, she sent him a pleading look. Amused, he gave her a little shrug. Her expression turned from pleading to desperation. Finally taking pity on her, he sauntered over.

"Excuse me, ladies, but I think it's time my wife had a little lie down. She's not used to the rigors of the hunt, and I worry that she might have overdone it today. Americans aren't used to the bracing country life like us."

Chora rolled her eyes but contented herself with only narrowing her eyes afterwards. A slow smile spread across her face. He experienced a moment of fear. "Landon, darling, wasn't it you who needed the nap after we spent the day at Disneyland?"

"Absolutely not."

"It was one of our first dates."

"Well then, maybe it wasn't Disneyland that made me tired. Maybe my fatigue had a different cause." Landon rather enjoyed watching her open and close her mouth as the women twittered around them. "If you'll excuse us." Without waiting for their consent, he reached out for Chora's hand and led her firmly away.

"You didn't play fair."

"I don't most of the time. Especially when I want something." A faint trace of pink darkened her complexion as she nibbled on her bottom lip. He wasn't sure what had caused the change, but he wasn't complaining. "And what I want now is to get as far away as possible from all these people."

"Really?" Her eyes softened as she looked up at him, a questioning look in her gaze.

"Yes. I'm exhausted from being surrounded by a crowd I can barely stand."

"Oh." The question vanished as quickly as it had appeared and was replaced with a slight shimmer, almost like she was sad. *Or hurt?*

Landon continued to walk them back to their rooms. "I want to apologize for this weekend." *Am I really sorry?* "I know it was a lot and, well, you've been terribly good about it all."

Chora nodded, not meeting his eyes. "It's all just part of our agreement. Hopefully we did a good job, and I can get back to my life and commitments in LA."

Landon wasn't sure he liked the sound of that as much as he should.

CHAPTER 14

The water was warm against his hand as Landon rinsed his razor. Finished, he stared at his reflection, inspecting his shave. In a matter of hours, he and Chora would be away from here and the constant scrutiny. It would be a relief to finally drop the charade and return to normal life again. *Wouldn't it?* Pushing the dangerously tantalizing thought of what it would be like to have Chora in his life as more than a friend and fake wife, he dried his hands. *Maybe I need to concentrate on convincing Grandpa instead of such frivolousness.*

Landon was still feeling slightly off kilter listening to the conversation swirl around him as he escorted Chora down for breakfast and joined the others at the table. "I am curious how you plan to manage your charity whilst being Landon's wife?" Grandpa asked with a deceptively casual tone.

Chora swallowed her scrambled eggs, choking at the unexpected attention. "Landon appreciates that I'm as passionate for my charity as he is for his work."

"You haven't exactly answered the question." To an

outsider, Uncle appeared bored, but Landon knew him better than that. He knew the cunning behind the question. The man was at his most dangerous.

"Well, of course, I will be spending my time between LA and wherever Landon is." Chora looked at Landon for confirmation.

"Exactly," he added. "For now, we are both desperate to spend as much time as possible together. We are, as you would expect, in the first flush of marriage."

"I think philanthropy is quite the suitable pursuit for someone who has married into Chora's situation." Grandmother smiled serenely across the table. Landon wasn't sure his grandmother would approve if she knew how hands-on she normally was. In fact, he was positive she'd be horrified at how far from the genteel fundraisers and tea parties she likely envisioned it all to be like.

Landon's mouth set in annoyance as he witnessed a long look between his grandfather and uncle. "But back to the original question, Grandfather. Chora will be running the charity remotely for a while longer as she will be joining me in Crete. I find that I can't bear the thought of being parted with her, even for a couple of weeks." He reached down, entangling her fingers with his. Her skin was cold against his as she smiled a little stiffly at him, but without disagreement. Satisfied that no more questions would be coming, Landon settled in for breakfast. Cook, after all, really did serve a superior table.

∿

HOW DARE HE! The eggs turned to rubber in Chora's mouth, suddenly as digestible as Landon's announcement. *He had no right to tell me where and what I am doing.* The truth niggled at her that somehow, since she'd landed in England, she'd allowed herself to think they were friends, that this was anything other than a business arrangement. One that he held all the power in.

She wasn't sure how long the breakfast stretched out for as guests came down and joined them, reminiscing about the weekend's hunt and extending invitations for future events. Finally, after what seemed like a lifetime, Landon began to make their farewells. At this point, Chora was amazed she hadn't chipped a tooth from the fixed smile adorning her face. The minute they were safely alone, she exploded.

"What do you call that?"

Landon's brows squished together. "What do I call what?"

"Don't play innocent with me," she hissed, stalking over to him. "Telling everyone that I'm off to Crete with you. I have absolutely no intentions of going there." Chora permitted herself a withering look. "You're not the only one who has a life to get back to. Unlike yours, mine actually is life and death."

Landon's stare turned coldly frigid. "Let me remind you that if we can't convince my grandfather that we are happily in love, then your animals will pay the price too. And right now, he isn't buying our act." He stepped slowly forward as he spoke until he drew level with her, so close she could feel the heat of his body. "Looks like you're coming to Crete with me whether you like it or not." Turning on his heel, he stormed toward the door. "I have to say goodbye to my friends. I suggest you are ready to leave when I come back." Without another word, he closed the door behind him, too much of a well-bred gentleman to slam it, although Chora suspected he was tempted.

Deflated, she sunk onto the bed. *I can't believe he's telling me.* He didn't even bother to make it seem like a request.

Sure, they had a deal, but it had felt like they were partners in crime, not him in charge and her following his orders like a good little girl.

Chora picked up the pillow and threw it at the door Landon had just gone through, wishing she'd had the forethought to do so when she'd had a chance of hitting him with it. Taking a deep breath, she began to dial the charity. *Might as well let them know I've been ordered to Crete.*

"Hello, Animals Are Forever."

The voice didn't sound familiar. *Surely no one new had started. I haven't been away that long.* "Who is this?"

"I'm Jessica. Whom am I speaking to?"

"Chora Davi—" She cringed at her lapse. "Chora Astley."

"Oh my gosh. I'm so sorry, I didn't know it was you."

"That's all right, Jessica. I don't think I've ever had the opportunity to meet you?" Chora left the question hanging.

"No, I haven't been here very long. In fact, today is my second day. They've got me answering the phones."

"Well, I thank you for volunteering. What made you decide to?" She was fascinated by all the different walks of life people who helped animals came from.

"I'm a veterinary student and I wanted to help." A pause. "I don't want to seem ungrateful, but I didn't think I would be playing receptionist."

Chora tried to stifle her sigh before it could be heard down the line as she rubbed the bridge of her nose. "To be honest, I would think there would be better uses of your skill than this, too. What did Christina say when she gave you the task?"

"I haven't met a Christina."

"Blonde? Nails that are completely unsuitable to working with animals?"

"Oh, I think I heard about her yesterday. At least, I think

it was about her. She met someone and quit. Apparently it was short notice, and a lot of the other girls here weren't very happy."

This time the sigh escaped her before she could stop it. "I see." *Darn it, Landon! I should be on my way home to deal with this mess.*

"But I'm sure you'll be back soon—or that's what I've been told." Jessica's voice trailed off.

Guilt fueled the fire of her anger at Landon. "Unfortunately, something has come up and I'm going to be delayed."

"Oh, um, well, I'm sure it can't be helped. Everyone will keep things going and you'll be back in no time."

Chora wasn't so sure.

❧

"WHAT I CAN'T bloody decide is if you're the bravest man I've ever met or the stupidest." Alistair peered at him as if the answer was somewhere on his face.

"I don't know what the fuss is about. Grandfather isn't one hundred percent buying the marriage, so I told her she needs to come to Crete. America will have to wait for her." His friends exploded into laughter, thumping each other on the back.

"You told her?" Freddy raised dubious brows. "I can imagine how well she took that." He paused, mouth dropping open in stunned surprise. "Old chap, don't tell me that the breakfast table was the first she'd heard about it?"

"Surely he's not that bloody stupid," Alistair said. "Or...?"

"He is that stupid," Stirling finished for him.

Landon's mouth puckered with annoyance. There was nothing wrong with how he'd handled it. Chora would understand it was nothing personal once she settled down. These howling loons weren't helping in the slightest. "I'm glad you lot are so clearly enjoying your stay here. However, Chora and I need to be on our way if we are to make good time to Heathrow." His dignity was somewhat tested by the chortles that followed him as he left the room. *So much for them being helpful.*

CHAPTER 15

It had taken reserves of strength that Chora hadn't known she'd possessed to remain in the role of loving wife while they flew over to Crete when all she wanted to do was glare at him for ruining her life. Maybe that was a more authentic version of marriage than what they had previously been engaged in.

Flying over the island, she'd been pulled from her sulk by the captivating view. The rugged coasts were crisscrossed with gorges and dotted with villages and coves, the high mountain ranges adorned with snow-capped peaks. There was a vitality to this island that verged on being a physical presence—and she hadn't even landed yet.

"I remember feeling the same way when I first saw it, too." Liveliness sparkled from Landon's eyes.

"So, now you're telling me I feel the same way as you? Should I wait for you to tell me when I need to use the bathroom, too?" she hissed at him, mindful that the stewardess was buckled into her seat at the end of the plane. *Gah, I sound like a peevish five-year-old.* Chora glared at him. It was his fault, after all, that she was acting like this. She turned back to stare out the window without an answer from him.

"Chora, I think you need to calm down," he said quietly, giving a smile over her shoulder at the crew. "We both have too much to lose now through irrational choices."

"Is that a suggestion or an order?" Her sweet smile was at odds with the frostiness of her words.

Landon raked his hands through his hair. It wasn't fair that his tousled hair made him look like a hot professor. "I'm sorry. Once we were alone, I should've asked and tried to respect your wishes as well. The reality is, I needed to make a snap decision before it all fell apart, and then it was too late to change it."

Despite herself, she softened ever so slightly. "I don't like being told what to do."

"I've noticed."

"I'm really needed back home."

"And I'm sorry that you can't be there, but if there is anything I can do to help, I will."

Chora hesitated, held fast still by the need to hold on to her irritation that was quickly deserting her. "I guess I can see where you were coming from, but it would've been nice to feel like it was a joint decision."

Landon nodded sagely, the ghost of a smile on his lips like a naughty child who knew he'd already been forgiven. "I promise not to do it again."

She wagged her finger at him. "Don't make promises you can't keep. Just talk to me afterwards." Chora watched the huge fortified ancient walls around the city come into view. "Now, tell me about Crete."

"Well, that's Heraklion and…"

❧

Names like Knossos and Zakros mingled and swirled with names of colleagues from the museum Landon had introduced Chora to as she joined him on the patio at his villa. The village he lived in was utterly charming. Somehow, she knew deep in her soul that, when this was all over, this is how she would remember Landon. The deeply contented man who waited for her expectantly, completely at ease in his surroundings.

Deep grooves appeared at the sides of his mouth when he saw her. "Welcome to what I consider my real home." Landon made a sweeping gesture to the food that was laid out on the table.

The fare was humbler than what had been offered in England, but Chora thought she'd never seen anything so delicious. "I didn't notice a butler when we arrived. Is it their day off?"

He tut-tutted her. "How quickly you've grown used to the finer things in life." Chora poked her tongue out at him. "I have a housekeeper who comes twice a week to clean, do my laundry, and make sure I have food. Other than that, I am completely on my own." He poured some wine into a pair of glasses. "I like it that way."

"I think I would, too." Movement at the edge of the patio where it joined a hedge caught her eye. "You never mentioned you had a dog."

"That's because I don't." Landon followed her line of sight. "He was here just before I left, skulking about the place."

"Does he belong to anyone?"

"It's possible, but there are lots of strays on the island."

Chora grabbed some cured meat from the table. Slowly, she inched her way forward. "Hey, gorgeous," she crooned. The dog didn't react. Emboldened, she went closer. "Are you hungry?" Chora held the meat out. This time she could see his tail firmly clamped down, the backbone jutted out through matted hide or what hide was left from the mange. Frosted eyes stared back at her, cloudy with age and cataracts. The dog's gray muzzle twitched. "You poor thing. You must be hungry."

Slowly, she squatted down, extending the food out. He might've once been someone's dog, but he hadn't been for a very long time. Inch by inch, he belly-crawled until he was as close as he dared, stretching to the very limits of his ability to ever so gently take the food. It stood as a testimony to his temperament that, even as mad with hunger as he must've been, he was still a gentleman.

"I think we should adopt him."

"I didn't think you were planning on staying in Crete for a moment longer than you absolutely needed to."

"I'm not, but you are." Chora kept her tone light and sing-songy so as not to startle the poor creature.

"It's a terrible idea. What would I do with him?" Landon's face was such a study of horrified protest that, under normal circumstances, it would've been funny.

"You care for him, make sure he's fed and has water and that he has a safe, dry, warm bed for his old bones. I think that's a pretty good starting place and one that a man with your means should more than amply be able to provide." She gave him a stern look over her shoulder. If he was half the man she thought he was, he would rise to the challenge.

"I don't even know what to call him."

"I'm sure he won't mind." She tried not to smile. Landon might still be in denial, but he'd just been adopted by a dog.

"Velchanos is one of the main Minoan gods," he offered hesitantly. "Similar to what Zeus would become."

"It sounds like a fine strong name. Velchanos," she said, trying it out. The dog licked her hand. "I think he likes it." Slowly, she stood and walked back to Landon, the hound staying with her until she drew level to her husband. Then, with slow arthritic movements, he laid himself down beside him. "I think you have a friend."

"I think I don't know what you're talking about."

Chora grinned into her wine. Clearly, Landon didn't think she could see him sneaking pieces of food down to his new dog. Her heart fluttered in her chest. After all, animals were the best judges of people.

Nothing had ever absorbed Landon the way the Minoans had. From learning of their existence to every shaded nuance since then, it had been his one constant passion. It had given him a sense of contentment that nothing else had ever come close to, and yet, now he'd made the startling realization that it could somehow be made deeper, more complex, by coming home to someone and discussing the day's work and to bounce ideas off. But Landon knew in his heart that it would only work if that someone was Chora. Somehow, she managed to shine her inner light until it lit up every aspect and left nothing hidden in the shadows. He'd insisted she come to Crete to continue the charade for Grandfather's benefit, but he'd also done it for himself.

Pushing the door to his villa open, Landon wasted no time in making his way to the back terrace where he knew he'd find her with maybe a book in hand, maybe her laptop, but always with the dog at her feet. *Well, until Velchanos sees me.* The hound would always rise as quickly as his old bones would let him, which was a little faster than it had been now that he had a full belly at all times and a soft bed to lay his head. The coat—once a thing that only the brave wanted to pat—was now becoming velvety.

Snagging a bottle of wine on the way through the

kitchen, he whistled happily, rolling up his shirt sleeve with his free hand as he pushed the door open with his back to the outside world. He stopped in his tracks. Where he had been expecting one woman he cared about, he now found two.

"Hello, Mother. I wasn't expecting you." Landon kissed each cheek before giving Chora a sound kiss on the mouth. *Obviously for Mother's benefit...*

"Landon, you know what I'm like. I like to live free as a bird. I was in Monaco, and suddenly I hear a whisper that the marquess, my son, has finally been caught. Well, you know I had to bloody well come here and find out the truth of it."

"Well, Mother, I can see that you have met my beautiful bride, Chora. Chora, I wish that Mother would've had the manners to let us know to expect her."

"Oh, don't worry about me." Chora's eyes were wide as she looked between them, seemingly starstruck by his parent. "You didn't tell me she was famous—or Australian."

"My best friend is actually the mother of Landon's best friend. We met when we first came to London to model. We'd never been out of Australia before that," Mother supplied helpfully.

"Alistair?" If possible, Chora's eyes grew wider.

"Of course. I take it that my darling son hasn't told you very much about me. I remember when his father and I were newly married. We didn't have much time for talking either. We had much more pleasant things on our minds." His mother gave him a naughty wink and laughed at the color fanning across Chora's cheeks.

"As you say, Mother, it rather hadn't come up in conversation." *But I have a strong suspicion that is all about to change.*

"Well, I'd hate for her to think you got your stuffiness from me. Your brilliance and that adventurous soul you have lurking under that tightly buttoned shirt is all from me." His mother raised a glass to the sky. "And I thank the gods for that!"

"You're nothing like what I imagined Landon's mother to be like." Chora's eyes shone with barely restrained intrigue. "Was his father like you, too?"

His mother spluttered her drink. "Good Lord, no! Well"— her eyes softened at some long-ago memory—"there was a glorious time when he was as free as the wind and, I believe, he was happy for the first time ever." Her eyes clouded. "But then he made his decision and threw away everything for his father."

Landon stared her. He knew the story—at least the bones of it. But suddenly it occurred to him that he'd never heard his mother's version straight from her lips. He poured himself a glass of wine and settled in. *When in Rome—or Crete, as the case may be—and all that.* "Perhaps Chora would like to hear how you and Father met?"

Chora beamed at him. Clearly, she'd been dying to know, but hadn't figured out how to ask. "Yes, please. I'd love to, as long as you don't think I'm intruding."

"Goodness me, girl, no. I'm Australian not bloody British. We'll tell you everything and throw in the shirt off our back at the same time."

"Mother, you might have noticed, can be a little dramatic," Landon muttered into his glass, earning himself a quelling look from the woman in question.

She flipped her hair. "Only when the occasion calls for it." She gave Chora a saucy wink. "And I've never found an occasion that didn't call for it."

"Mother, don't teach Chora any of your secrets. I find her quite delightful exactly the way she is." His wife laughingly waved off his compliment, but he did notice the stain of pink that brightened.

"Such a party pooper." His mother made a face at him

before taking a sip of her wine. "Now, how I met Philip, Landon's father ... well, it all began with the trip of a lifetime. My parents were quite eccentric. Brilliant, but eccentric. Daddy was a lecturer at a university back in Australia and taught philosophy and English literature, and Mummy wrote poetry, and they were both madly in love with each other. They were until the day they died, which incidentally was only two days apart. Our house always had academics and artists coming in and out of it. The kettle was always on, and I don't think I can remember a single moment of silence growing up. As a teenager, I posed for several of those artists, and one of them used photography as his medium. He had taken pictures of all the famous models of the fifties and sixties. Well, the next thing I know, I'm on a plane and headed to London. The agency set me up in a shared room with another model who had arrived the week before me."

"Alistair's mother?" Chora guessed.

"Alistair's mother, Donna. She came from a pastoral family in the outback, and just before she came over, her father had discovered a large deposit of iron ore. I think if they'd known how wealthy they were about to become, they wouldn't have let her come over to London by herself." His mother shrugged "Or maybe, knowing Donna, they wouldn't have been able to stop her."

Landon found himself drawn into her story. He pictured a younger version of her, suitcase at her feet, meeting Donna for the first time. "I'm not sure London would've known what had hit it with the two of you."

"Oh, my darling. It was such a magical time. We worked hard and then partied even harder. We traveled and met people who amazed us with their brilliance. It was such a terribly wonderful time to be young and beautiful and alive. One day, we were invited to a gathering for one of our friends—he was going to read some poetry—and I saw this man. My goodness, he was gorgeous. He was dressed terribly properly and stood to one side, but every word my friend read seemed to strike a chord in him." His mother's gaze drifted off into a memory. "I simply had to meet him. We talked about poetry, of which I was quite able to do thanks to Mummy, and he told me his name was Philip."

Such a wonderful longing filled her voice for a man that, in his lifetime, Landon had never seen this side of. Such a polar opposite was this man to the cold, proper brusque man who had periodically visited him at boarding school that he wondered if his mother had somehow cast him forth from her fruitful imagination.

"That summer, we read poetry to each other and laughed, and yes, we became lovers."

"Mother!" Landon was scandalized that she would so openly admit it.

"Oh, Landon. We were young and in love." She gave him a knowing look. "I rather imagine you know exactly what I'm talking about." He found himself growing warm under her scrutiny. Sheepishly, he glanced at Chora, her words a lot closer to the mark about some of his fantasies than he wanted to admit. "And then we found out we were pregnant with you and we decided to run away and get married. I was naïve, I guess. It never occurred to me to ask about his family. I knew he was well off—you could tell just by hearing him speak—but we were so wrapped up in each other that it never seemed to come up."

"What happened?" Chora asked anxiously, reaching for her wineglass.

"Well, the fantasy had to end at some point." His mother's voice was ruthlessly blunt. "We got married and, a couple of weeks later, word must've gotten to his parents. We were summoned. And I gather you've met them—it's not exactly a warm, fuzzy welcome, and doubly so for the wanton Aussie who had ensnared their son. His father offered me a million dollars to abort Landon and walk away." Landon could only stare at her. He'd never heard this before, but she wore about her such a wounded sadness enmeshed with pride that he had no reason to doubt her. "Philip stood firm. We were his family—me, you, still not even born yet. Stupidly, I thought we would be able to weather the storm, and we did for a while."

His mother fiddled with the stem of her glass.

"Four years." Bitterness twisted her mouth. "Four years is all it took for that hateful old man to turn Philip away from everyone who truly loved him. But maybe I need to apportion more of the blame to Philip as well. He was the one, after all, who ultimately made his choice. First, he took away Philip's allowance that was his due as first son, and then we were kicked out of his townhouse. It was hard for Philip. He'd never anticipated that he would work. All he'd ever wanted to do was write poetry and manage the estates. He looked for work, but it was difficult with no skills. I was able to get the odd modeling job, but I was a mother to a young child now. My life was completely different. Finally, I came home one day, and Philip told me it was all over. He held a check out to me for a million dollars. I threw it to the ground and told him it was worthless compared to him. Philip told me his mind was made up, I had to understand that it would never last, that we were too different. At last, he turned cold to my pleading and then the truth. He had been given an ultimatum between losing his title and inheritance or me. I asked him how he could turn his back on his wife, his child, and that is when he broke me. He told me that you would remain with him. I railed at him. I might have even clawed, but he was immovable."

"Now that is what I would expect from Father," Landon murmured. *Cold, hateful.*

"I was able to see Landon a few times a year. The nanny would bring him to our meetings, and I watched as the happy, joyous little boy I loved was hardened into the same empty cold shell as the rest of them."

"That's horrible." Landon was surprised to see Chora dabbing at her eyes. His wife had such a tender heart.

"It got better once I went to boarding school," he offered, his mother rewarding him with a grateful smile. "At least we could visit without always being watched."

"That's true. But I always felt sorry for your nanny. She truly seemed like a nice woman put in a terrible position. I was always thankful you had her in your life." She seemed to will the sadness from her, determined not to linger in past pain. "Now, my darling, tell me what you think of Crete. It is, after all, my son's other great love."

Solemnly, Chora gazed around her. "It's unlike anything I've ever experienced. There's a hint of old magic maybe, like a whisper I can't quite hear." She lowered her lashes as if embarrassed by her whimsy. Landon's heart sang at her words. He reached down to pat at the old dog that was settled at his feet.

"If you really want to experience it, come with me." He gave Velchanos a final scratch before returning his gaze to Chora. "I think we can leave Mother in the protection of this faithful hound." The dog in question gave a loud snore, setting them all to laughing.

"If you don't think we're abandoning you?" Chora asked carefully.

"Don't rush back on my account." Mother waved them off. "I find tonight I want to remember how things were, not how they ended."

Sympathetically, he smiled at her, not sure what, if anything, he could say to ease the sorrow shadowing her face. Rising, he held his hand out to Chora. "My lady."

"My lord." She playfully gave a curtesy. "Now that I've agreed to come, are you going to tell me where you're taking me?"

Landon waved at his mother and led Chora through the house and toward his car. "No, but I will tell you that it is only a short drive."

"Have I ever told you that I have a mean husband?"

"No, because I know for a fact that he's quite the gentleman."

"Is that a fact?"

"Yes." He nodded solemnly at her, enjoying the banter. "Terribly handsome, too."

"I've heard that rumor. He also smells nice, for what it's worth. But I have to let you in on a little secret." Chora leaned in close as he opened the car door for her. "We try not to let him know as he is insufferable at the best of times." With a merry little giggle, she climbed up into her seat and closed the door firmly behind her, leaving him to stare at where she had stood.

Blinking, a slow smile spread over his face as he made his way to the other side of the car. *Saucy little minx.*

THE STONE SHIMMERED as the lights at the base of the buildings shone on them. The ruins had taken on a magical glamour in the twilight. "What you see glimmering is unique to buildings on the island. It's attributed to the extensive use of selenite from the local quarries." Landon loved the awestruck way she stared at Knossos Palace. "When it was first constructed, it would've been a remarkable sight, quite unlike anything that had ever been seen in Crete."

"I can imagine," she breathed. "Do we know what destroyed it?

"We believe that Knossos was destroyed sometime in the 1300s BC by fire."

"What happened to the Minoans? Did they build somewhere else?"

Goodness, I love her inquiring mind. If he was honest with himself, it was only part of the whole that he admired. *Admired? Could it be more?* His mind danced nimbly away from that thought. "They remained on the island, but it was the beginning of the decline for them, and the civilization finally collapsed by 1200 BC."

"But what majesty they left behind them." Chora's eyes shimmered as brightly as the selenite surrounding her. Landon found it impossible to look away.

He cleared his throat. "There are some rooms I'd like to show you." He led her through the winding ruins that wrapped around the central courtyard, columns still stretching to the sky as they ascended a grand staircase, shield frescos lining the walls. "According to Greek mythology, the famous architect, Daedalus, designed the palace with such complexity that none who entered could find their way out."

Landon swore he heard her whisper "I know the feeling," but he couldn't be sure.

They passed through a massive door. Inside, a stone purification tank stood to one side, and to the other was a throne guarded by twin griffin frescos. "This is the King's Chamber."

"Landon, it's like you can feel the power of this room." She rubbed her arms. "I have goosebumps."

As if bound together, his own flesh pimpled. "Sometimes, when I'm working, it almost feels like the very rock has absorbed the history." He rubbed the back of his neck. "That sounds silly now that I've said it aloud."

"No, Landon." Chora stepped closer, reaching out to

touch his arm. The instant they connected, electricity shot through him. He looked at her stunned to find her staring at him, mouth slightly open, eyes wide. *Surely she hadn't felt it, too.* She licked her lips, tongue darting nervously out from her parted lips. "I don't think it's silly at all. When we first met, when we agreed to our—" Chora paused. Landon was painstakingly aware of where her hand still rested. "—arrangement, I thought you were cold and abrupt. But now, I can't believe I ever thought that of you. There's a passion inside you that's breathtaking." She made to withdraw her hand, but Landon wouldn't allow this woman to slip from his grip so easily.

He snared her around her slender waist and pulled her in tightly to him for fear that somehow this moment would disappear into the balmy evening air. *It's you,* his mind screamed, but his tongue remained mute. Slowly, he lowered his head. If his lips could not say it, then they could show her. It was more than a kiss. His mouth caressed hers with an exquisite tenderness. Inside, his mind battled with his heart. *Don't get attached,* it commanded. *Just because you have changed, don't forget the arrangement still stands. It will all be over soon, and it will only be a memory like this room.* His heart wept, recognizing the truth of his mind.

CHAPTER 16

Chora felt warm all over and an odd, giddy rush went through her as she thought about last night's kiss. Unbidden, her fingers stole to her mouth, to touch where his lips had been. She didn't want to think about the possible explanation for why it had so affected her, but there was still no escaping it. It wasn't like they hadn't kissed before. But this time it had felt different, real. *What would it be like for Landon to really be my husband?* She glanced at her watch, trying to distract herself from her nagging inner thoughts and turmoil.

"I'm sorry, am I boring you?" Landon's mother asked dryly.

Chora cringed, knowing her face was already flushed. "No, it's nothing like that. I really do like spending time with you and getting to know you." It was true, it was rather nice having some girl time while Landon was at work.

Laughter tinkled from the older woman. "It's all right, I was only teasing you. It actually makes me really happy to see my daughter-in-law counting down the hours till her husband comes home. Especially after last night."

Chora's face felt like it was about to go up in flames. "Oh, it wasn't like that. Or maybe a little?" She gave up with a chuckle of her own.

"Landon hasn't known a loving family. It's always been my hope that he would find one of his own." She stared down at her empty hands. "I've always felt guilty for the example we'd set for him. When his father and I got divorced, custody was dragged through the courts, and I felt such anger at Philip for abandoning me and it felt that he was somehow punishing me by trying to take our son away from me." Pity for the other woman filled Chora as she locked gazes with her, regret starkly staring back. "Landon's grandparents are very proper, and by then Philip had changed so much I didn't recognize him as the man I'd fallen in love with. It wasn't exactly what a child needs, and then his father died. For the longest time, I think all Landon's ever loved is history. It's like a puzzle he gnaws away at, trying to solve. It's also safe. There's no risk of him having to open up."

A shiver of remembrance danced up Chora's spine. Last night, somehow history and magic had seemed intertwined into something new, deeper. *It most certainly hadn't felt safe.*

Landon's mother thankfully didn't see her reaction, reaching down to give Velchanos a scratch on his head. "With you, I see him starting to thaw and show a softer side." She reached out and gave Chora's hand a squeeze. "Thank you. It means that I'm not needed here. It's really the only reason I came, to see if my boy was going to be all right, and he is." She made to stand.

"What, right now? What about Landon? Don't you want to wait for him to come home and say goodbye?' Chora was caught off-guard at the sudden announcement.

"Landon and I do best without goodbyes. The ones we had when he was younger were too traumatizing for both of us. Now, you—I want you to promise to not be a stranger and visit me often with that son of mine." Her expression turned naughty. "And don't make me wait too long for grandchildren."

A strangled sounding laugh escaped Chora. "Ah, um, that's not really something we've discussed." *We are so far from baby making.*

"His grandfather will expect it, and best hope that the first one is a bloody boy. Honestly, it was the one thing I bloody did right." Her face softened. "But I do wonder what a little girl would've been like. As much as I'd like the old man to not always get his way, children really are a gift."

A little girl with her father's piercing eyes and fierce intelligence. Chora shook the thought from her mind. "I do like children," she admitted.

"Well, that's a start." The older woman's eyes were much like her son's, Chora realised with a start as they twinkled kindly at her. "Now, give me a hug." A sense of loss hit her that she would probably never see the woman again. She felt like she could have been close to this fascinating being who had lived her life, for the most part, on her terms, except for the one thing she'd lost. *The simple arrangement kept getting more tangled up the longer it went on.* Chora didn't know whether she should feel relieved or saddened that the time was steadily ticking by.

IT HAD BEEN nice having Mother visit for a couple of days, but Landon rather enjoyed having Chora all to himself again. *Well, shared with Velchanos.* It was just a terribly nice way to live, and it had to do with the amazing woman who waited for him at the end of each day. It still boggled his mind how easily Chora had fit in with life in Crete. Sure, she probably preferred to be back in LA seeing to her charity, but not once had she mentioned it *after* the initial hoo-ha back in England. Landon had little doubt that it had made things more difficult for her being there.

Pulling into the entrance of the villa, irritation made him glare at the ringing phone, his uncle's number flashing. *Just like a Band-Aid, it was always best to just get it over with.* "Hello, Uncle."

"Hello, Nephew. How is life in Crete treating you and your little bride?" His smarmy tone set Landon's teeth on edge.

"It is as perfect as I imagined." *That wasn't true. It was more than I ever imagined.*

"I highly doubt that on your boring little island. But don't you worry, I just so happen to be cruising near you. A friendly sheik I know has graciously offered me use of his megayacht. You should join me."

"I'd rather not." Landon would rather have a root canal than set foot in that viper's nest.

"Oh, is there trouble in paradise?" his uncle asked in a silken voice.

"No, but we're much to ensconced in our rustic life here as newlyweds." *Truth.*

"Oh, please. There's no need to keep trotting out the newlywed card. It just seems to the family that you married this girl terribly conveniently, paraded her at one gathering, and then sequestered her away. It might appear—and I'm not the one saying it, you understand, but to others it might appear that you have something to hide." The words hung heavy, threatening, between them.

"Fine," he ground out ungraciously. "Chora and I accept your invitation."

"Oh, how lovely. I'll make the arrangements to collect

you." Relieved, Landon heard the click of the phone. At least he'd been spared his uncle's gloating. Sighing, he opened the car door and stepped out. Now he had to break it to Chora. *Great.*

He stopped to admire the sight of Chora singing ever so slightly out of tune to Velchanos as he waited patiently to be fed. Landon would never get used to the luminosity that seemed to come from within her, filling a room with a sweet brightness. She scooped ladles of homemade food into a dish and added dashes of powders and slurps of fish oil. Judging from the ropes of drool hanging from the old hound's mouth, the anticipation was extreme. Never once did he take his eyes off her. At last, he was rewarded for his diligent patience when she placed the revered plate in front of him.

"Oh." Chora jumped when she saw him. "I didn't hear you come in."

"I heard singing and didn't want to interrupt." He loved how she blushed, embarrassed to have been caught.

"Velchanos likes it." She raised her chin in defiance.

"So do I."

"Oh." Her eyes softened, a questioning gaze seeking his own. "You have impeccable timing. You have just enough time to wash up before dinner."

"I'm not the only one with impeccable timing," he muttered sourly under his breath, remembering his promise to his uncle.

Her brows furrowed. "Did you say something?"

Landon sighed. His family had a habit of making him do that. "My uncle has invited us to join him on a little cruise. He just so happens to be sailing off the coast of Crete."

Chora shook her head in a slow back and forth sweep of denial. "No. No-no. No, thanks."

"My sentiments exactly." Before he could clarify, a relieved smile broke out over her face. He felt like such a jerk now that he'd have to correct her assumption. "However, it wasn't so much an invitation as a velvet-gloved demand. Unfortunately, I had to accept."

"Oh, Landon, but he's such a horrible toad of a man." She giggled. "And that's being offensive to toads."

"Well, you can keep your amphibians. I'll stick to dogs, hey, Velchanos?" He smiled to where the dog, having wolfed down his meal, had now lain down. Something didn't seem quite right. "Velchanos?" he said slightly louder as he stepped closer. Dread closed around his heart when he found no sign of movement.

Chora knelt beside Velchanos, softly stroking his fur, her hand resting on his ribcage. "I'm sorry, Landon, but he's gone." Sadness choked her voice. A chill settled over him, and the sight of tears spiking her lashes compounded the grief with guilt as she wiped her eyes. "At least he was happy and safe at the end." He watched as a droplet fell from her eyes onto the fur of the old dog.

This was why it was best not to care about anything or anyone. "It was a stupid idea to adopt him anyway. I never should've let you talk me into it." Somehow it was safer to direct anger at Chora than to dwell on the wretchedness that tugged at him.

Chora stared at him with hurt-filled eyes, evidence of her desolation still clearly evident, making his inner torment worse. "How can you say that? Every animal deserves to be loved and cared for. What we were able to give to Velchanos, I was honored to do it for him." A sob escaped her. "I wish I could do it for all of them."

"It's why you married me, isn't it?" he replied in reckless anger. Bitterly, he couldn't stop himself from lashing out, not caring that it was an arrangement where he'd been the one to propose to her. And that was the crux of it, wasn't it? She wasn't with him because she cared about him. It was because he was a means to an end.

The look she cast his way sent ice crystalizing through his stomach. Wordlessly, she spun on her heel and fled, leaving him to his lonely remorse as he gave his dog the burial he deserved.

CHAPTER 17

Somehow, when Velchanos had died, the Landon she'd started to have feelings for had disappeared too. Remote, cold and locked so far within himself—Chora didn't know what he was even thinking anymore. As they boarded his uncle's yacht, she took his proffered arm, giving him a warning glance. They had come too far for him to ruin it all now.

Once onboard, semi-naked women lounged everywhere, the yacht stupendously immense. Chora made a note not to touch anything, and she was most definitely not going anywhere near the two jacuzzies she spied. "Ah, Landon, I see you've finally managed to tear yourself away from your dusty old ruin. And I don't mean the wife." The women closest to him giggled inanely as he smirked.

"I didn't realize we were coming to Silicon Valley," Chora retorted with a pointed glance at his company.

"Feisty. I know I've always liked that in a woman, but I think you'll find my nephew a little dull for your tastes. If you ever get bored, you know where to find me." She suddenly had the overwhelming urge to go bathe in an entire bottle of disinfectant.

"Uncle, if you ever speak to my wife like that again, I can promise you being bored will be the least of your worries." Landon's voice was coolly disapproving, at odds with the harshness of his threat. Chora stared out over the sparkling water, wishing she was anywhere but here.

"Calm down, old chap, I was only having a little fun. Ah —" He tapped the end of his nose. "Do I sense trouble in paradise? I hope the two of you aren't having a silly little lovers' tiff. Father would be so disappointed to hear that this love match isn't working out."

"We lost our dog yesterday." Chora narrowed her eyes, already regretting giving him more fodder.

"Is that all? Go get yourself another one. No need to be all down in the doldrums. Both of you are bringing the vibe down." He snagged some champagne glasses from a passing-by waiter. "Have some champagne. I was led to believe by my first wife, rest her soul, that the more expensive it is, the better it works. Or maybe it will make things worse. Who knows?" He gave them a sly sideways look. Not knowing what else to do, Chora took the glass from him.

"I'm amazed you even remember her. If I remember correctly, you only remained interested in her long enough to get your sons. How are they, by the way?" Landon casually sipped his champagne, brow raised in bored inquiry.

Chora didn't catch the reply, her complete attention suddenly focused on a horrifyingly familiar blonde figure. Heart pounding in her ears, she could only stare, silently praying that she was mistaken. As the woman turned, Chora didn't know whether to laugh, cry, or vomit—possibly a combination of all three. *Of all the megayachts sailing around the Mediterranean, why did Christina have to turn up on mine?*

"Excuse me," Chora interrupted. "I think I need to go

powder my nose." Without waiting for a reply, she headed inside, trying to sort out what she was going to do. Dimly, she was aware that Christina had followed her. Giving up, she turned around, ready to confront her problem head on.

"Hello, Christina. Fancy seeing you here."

"Imagine my surprise. But I've always found that, when I need it, I'm lucky." Christina smiled at her, her eyes somehow coldly assessing despite her smile. Long, pale pink nails wrapped around the stem of her glass, giving Chora the impression of claws around a heart.

"I only just found out that you'd left Animals Are Forever when I called to check in. Why didn't you at least call to say goodbye?"

"If you'd come back like you were meant to—or better still, not married my billionaire—you'd have known." Christina fluffed her pale blonde hair about her shoulders. "But as you can see, I managed to snare one for myself. It only took a few disgusting dates before the matchmaker got it right for me. Can you imagine? She tried to set me up with millionaires. As if! But now I've struck gold in more than one way, if you know what I mean. Or I will be very soon now that I've seen you."

Chora stared at the woman. She made it all sound so clinically impersonal. But isn't that what she'd done with Landon? *Except I never set out to trap him. We just kinda found each other when we needed it.* "I'm happy for you. Who's the lucky man?"

"His name's Charles. This is his yacht."

Chora could only stare at Christina horrified. *This just kept getting worse.* "Older English guy?" she clarified. *Who knew? Maybe there was more than one onboard.*

"Yes, that's him, and I believe you're married to his nephew." Christina's eyes glowed with triumph, filling Chora with dread with what was to come next.

"If you marry him, does that make you my aunt-in-law?" It wasn't much, but it did give her some pleasure in tweaking the other woman's nose. "Oh, and by the way, I don't know what he's told you, sweetie, but this isn't his yacht, it's just on loan. And he isn't a billionaire." *Not if I can do anything about it.*

Christina waved her observations away. "That actually leads me to an interesting thought. Are you still pretending to be married to the nephew?"

And there it was. "No, we're really married." She knew it was no use protesting, but she had to try.

"Well, it's a marriage of convenience, if I remember correctly. And believe me, I do, since it could've so easily been me instead of you." Pure ice trickled down Chora's spine. "Now, if my memory serves me right, he has to settle down to claim his inheritance, otherwise the old man is going to give it to his uncle, who I now just so happen to be dating."

Maybe she could brazen it out. "I don't know what you're talking about."

"We both know you do." Chora's mouth went dry. "Now, here's what I'm thinking. I can keep my mouth shut, but it's going to cost you. A lot. About one million dollars to be precise. That's just to begin with. Once your darling husband gets his inheritance, I'll want another fifty million."

"But I don't have that kind of money." Chora felt a nauseating sinking of despair.

"See, I also know that's not true. I made sure to check where all that money suddenly came from at the charity before I left. Landon gave you money as a down payment, if you will, didn't he? Smart girl. It's always best to get payment upfront."

"But as you just said, I gave it to the charity."

"How selfish of you. Take it back, or ask hubby dearest

for more. I don't really care where you get it from because, if you don't, I'm going to tell Charles, and I'm sure he will be very grateful."

Chora's chin trembled as she nodded. *What had she done?*

~

No matter how much Landon tried to fight how he felt about Chora—to push her away—he never could manage to actually drive her from his thoughts. *If losing Velchanos had hurt, how would he be able to breathe once she was gone?* Standing here on this floating palace full of fake people, all he wanted to do was whisk her away from here and return back to the magic that had been their time in Crete.

Thankfully, his uncle had gotten distracted when a pneumatically enhanced peroxide blonde had sauntered up, draping herself about him like a scarf. Something about the way she'd looked at him had made the hairs on the back of his neck stand up. Even though the sun hung low in the sky, it was suddenly chilly. When Chora had appeared, alarm immediately had him walking toward her. Anxiously, he scanned her face, her glow dulled to the point of nonexistence. None of the casual observers loitering nearby would have noticed, but they didn't know her the way he did.

"Are you all right?" he asked her in a low voice, careful that no one else should hear.

"I need to talk to you." Her lips were pressed tightly together before she even uttered the words. Landon could feel his heart rate increasing.

"Darling," he said in a loud voice, projecting it in his uncle's direction. "I'm tired, and I know you were exhausted from our day before we arrived. I think we should retire to our stateroom and have dinner sent there."

His uncle gave Chora a lascivious look, earning a glare

from the woman at his side. "That champagne working after all? It won't be the first time someone has a second honeymoon onboard."

Quickly, Landon led his wife away, locating a steward to show them to their room. Not fast enough for his liking, he finally closed the door behind him. Looking out the window, he saw the last sliver of light gleaming on the horizon. "Now, do you want to tell me what this is all about?"

"You remember how I wasn't actually the woman you were meant to go on that date with?"

"Yes, it was a Crystal? No, Christine?" He was baffled why they were even talking about someone he'd never met. If he had, he'd have never met the amazing woman in front of him…

"It's Christina. Anyway, after that date, I told her about your business proposal and then, obviously, she knew when we went through with it and got married." Chora stared down at her tightly clasped hands. "Now she's dating your uncle and it gets worse. She wants fifty million dollars or she's going to tell him."

Landon glared at her with burning, reproachful eyes. "How could you tell her?"

"Well, in the beginning, I had no intention of going through with it." *Why was she looking at him like he was in the wrong?* "And you told your friends."

"Friends. People I could trust with my life. Not some random gold digger. Is this woman your friend? Because if she is, I don't think much of your choice in friends."

Her head jerked back, and with a muffled cry, she stormed from the room. His blood still coursing through his veins, he marched after her, fired up with the need to continue the argument. Chora finally stopped at the bow of the yacht, miraculously free of lounging people. Without thought, he grabbed her by the elbow and spun her around.

"Is that what you think about me?" she screamed at him. "That I'm a gold digger?"

"I didn't say you were. I called your friend that. The friend who's about to ruin everything."

"Let me go." She struggled to pull herself free, but Landon wasn't ready to release her.

"That moment of stupidity is going to cost us everything." *It might already have.*

With one last tremendous effort, Chora wrenched herself free. No longer held up by him, she staggered backwards, trying to gain her balance. Too late, he desperately reached out to steady her, but she pushed his hands away in her anger. He saw in her eyes the moment she realized she was going to topple over the side of the yacht, the exact instance she went from trying to get away to pleading with him to save her, and then she was gone, plunging into the inky depths of the Aegean Sea.

Primal instinct kicked in and he was diving in after her before he'd drawn in another breath, the water jarring as he kicked his feet, pushing himself to greater depths, hand desperately outstretched, trying to grasp her. Touch alone was the only sense left to him in the darkness. By some miracle, hair knotted around his hand and, holding on tightly, he pulled her to the surface.

As he breached and sucked in breath, he cradled her head on his shoulder and called out, flailing his arm to attract the attention of the crew. He didn't know what god smiled down on him that night—maybe more than one—but somehow, despite the odds, they did.

It was only later when she was safe that what happened next played through his mind in a series of flashbacks as though, in the moment, he'd been unable to process and at the same time be able do what needed to be done. Getting her back on the deck. Performing CPR with a stranger until she spewed great geysers of salty water. Holding her as though his life depended on it while he rained kisses down on her as a faceless crowd watched on. Getting heli-lifted off the yacht as he held on to her hand like he would never let go, knowing how close he'd come to losing the one truly irreplaceable thing he'd ever had in his life. And then replaying again and again, until sleep claimed him as he watched over her in hospital, the terror-stricken moment when in the midnight waters he'd thought he'd lost her. *It would happen soon enough.*

CHAPTER 18

Chora's usually tanned skin looked paler than usual, her inner glow almost snuffed out. Remorse gnawed at Landon, knowing he was the cause as he stared down at her lying in the hospital bed. He'd spent a sleepless night clutching her hand. The few times he'd slowly drifted off, dreams that he knew would plague him for the rest of his life had haunted him, and he'd woken grasping at the air as if trying to catch something or someone in vain, fear holding him fast in its grip as he struggled to breathe.

Even now as he watched her slowly chew her breakfast, taking delicate sips of tea, unease grew in him, like any moment she might disappear into thin air, merely a mirage. "Lady Astley?" A doctor popped his head in the door. "I hear you had quite the adventure last night."

Chora gave him a slight smile. "It seemed like the easiest way to leave a party I didn't want to be at."

"Drastic, but efficient. But I don't know if my heart could take it again." Landon tried to keep his tone light, although he meant every word. *Last night, he'd almost lost his heart.*

"Well, as your medical professional, I'd strongly advise

that you don't do it again. If only for the sake of your husband." The doctor gave her a wink. "Now, I need to check a few things and, hopefully, if you pass and promise me you won't try to drink the entire Aegean Sea again, I think we should be able to discharge you today."

"I'll try my best." Her words were light, but Chora still didn't seem herself. Perhaps he should expect it after the harsh words that were exchanged yesterday added to the trauma of almost dying. A person was bound to be a little out of sorts. He raked his fingers through his hair, aware of his disheveled state. Landon wasn't sure how to even begin to make things better.

"I'll go get a coffee and give you some privacy. Would you like something, Chora?" *Me?* The words hung heavy between them.

Her gaze dropped to the steaming cup of tea she still clasped in her hands. "I'm fine, thank you." Landon tried not to read too much into it, but it was hard to not feel like he'd been dismissed.

Stopping along the way to ask a nurse for directions, he finally found himself fumbling with the coffee machine. Landon wasn't sure if what he was watching fill his paper cup was even worthy of the title, but beggars didn't have the luxury of being choosers. A message pinging through on his phone distracted him from his brewing thoughts. They'd been summoned home by Grandfather. *Obviously, the game was up. Her little friend and Uncle must have run straight to his grandparents.* And yet his heart was thrilled knowing he'd been granted a reprieve and had somehow been given more time with his wife.

～

THEY'D SAT opposite each other for the flight home and were now so close beside each other in the car that all Landon had to do was reach his hand out and he would be able to touch Chora's thigh, yet the distance between them had never felt greater. He found himself praying for traffic jams, detours, anything that would delay what he knew was waiting for them at his grandparent's estate. As soon as the axe hanging over their heads dropped, she would return to LA and out of his life forever. For what possible need would she have to ever return to Crete? To him?

The only bright spot to come out of all this was that he was eternally grateful he'd been able to give her the money at the very beginning. Knowing that it would help so many animals in need meant that it hadn't all been for nothing. *It never was*, his mind whispered. *You got Chora, if only for a moment.* Landon hoped that Chora's friend would be able to fundraise and help her continue what she was called to do. For himself, Crete would still be there. He might not be able to fund the work as he had—maybe he could try fundraising himself—but he would still find a way to pursue his passion. *Alone.*

The estate loomed large before him as he finally admitted to himself that he'd run out of time. Pulling up, he drew in a deep breath. "Chora," he began.

"Landon," she interrupted. "You don't have to say anything. I'm sorry. I know I messed up." Miserably, she stared down at her hands. "I wish I could take it all back. I never meant for this to happen." Her voice choked up.

"Chora, I don't blame you. I think maybe fate has a funny sense of humor. Regardless of what happens in there, I'm thankful I got to do it all with you." She stared at him, a question in her eyes. One that he'd give anything to answer, if only he was brave enough. The door being opened by the butler shattered the moment. *What was it with butlers and crumby timing?* Making his way around to her side, he held his hand out to her for what may be the final time. "Shall we?"

She smiled at him, her eyes shadowed with sadness. "We shall."

Landon tried not to think that the warmth of her hand in his would soon be nothing but a memory as they made their way into the house, following the butler even though there was no need to. A meeting like this would only take place in one setting—Grandfather's library.

Landon forced his feet to continue propelling him to the room, the slight smile not once slipping from his face when he saw his uncle and that ghastly blonde woman already firmly ensconced near the fire. "So nice of you to finally make it, Nephew."

"We were somewhat otherwise engaged," Landon responded, making sure Chora was comfortably seated before sitting himself beside her. As soon as he was settled, his fingers once again found their way to becoming entangled with hers. "As you are well aware of."

"There are a lot of things I'm now well aware of thanks to my new friend." The blonde smirked at them—or at least that's what he thought she was doing. It was almost impossible to tell with all the Botox and fillers.

"Which is why I've requested you come home." Grandfather at last joined the conversation, turning his chair around to face them at his desk. Grandmother hovered at his side. "Charles has brought me some quite serious allegations about the nature of your marriage. I would like to hear your side as I understand he has a vested interest in this as well and may not be entirely impartial."

Landon returned his stare coolly. "I would like to hear what he has to say first as I'm not entirely sure what I'm defending myself and Chora from."

"Oh please, Landon," his uncle sneered. "Just make it easier for us all and admit it."

"You want to know the nature of my marriage to Chora?" Landon pivoted ever so slightly so his words could be directed at his wife. "She is a gift I didn't know I was seeking and most assuredly did not deserve. But I'm not selfless enough to not be thankful every day that she somehow agreed to take this crazy leap of faith and agree to be my wife. She is more precious an achievement to me than deciphering Linear A. She is my Minoan Queen." There was a suspicion of moisture in Chora's eyes.

"Give it up already," whined the blonde. "For goodness' sake, you don't have to lay it on so thick. It's enough to make me sick."

"That's right," Uncle agreed. "Why don't you tell them what you know?"

Christina turned to address his grandfather. "Like I was telling you before they arrived, I used to work for Chora."

"At her animal charity?" Grandmother asked softly.

"Yes, and I know she was having some money troubles or something. Like, someone ran off and took all the money she had fundraised."

"She must have been distraught." Landon was surprised that, so far, only his grandmother had asked any questions.

"I guess so. Anyway, I'd joined this matchmaker service and when I finally got a match, I got a cold. Now, if I canceled the date, I wouldn't get a chance to meet any other billionaires."

"And that's important to you?" Grandmother encouraged.

"Well, who wants to be poor their whole life? Not me. So, I get Chora to fill in for me. Next thing I know, she's married my date! My billionaire!" Her voice rose alarmingly.

"But tell her what she told you after that first date," Charles encouraged her.

Christina gripped Landon's uncle's thigh tightly with her taloned hand. Frankly, Landon was surprised he wasn't wincing under the pressure. "She told me that he'd offered her money to pretend to be married to him. She was all high and mighty about it, too." She smirked at Chora. "Not so high and mighty now."

"So, you're saying they aren't really married?" Finally, Grandfather joined the fray.

"Yes."

"That's incorrect. I've seen their marriage certificate myself." Grandfather stared her down. Landon wasn't exactly sure what was going on, but it wasn't turning out the way he'd expected—or his uncle, for that matter.

"Well, I guess they got the silly piece of paper, but it's not a real marriage. They don't even share the same bed." Christina turned to Charles for support.

"They did here." Grandmother calmly took a sip from her china teacup.

"That's impossible," Charles snapped.

"Be very careful, Charles. You might be my son, but I won't allow you to talk to your mother like that," Grandfather said sternly. "You don't think we didn't verify the status of Landon's marriage for ourselves, especially with everything that was at stake? Do you think we're fools?" Landon prayed he was never on the receiving end of a look like that.

"No, Father, I didn't say that." Charles backpedaled.

"I would suggest you stop talking and listen. Landon and his wife have been under surveillance for some time, and we have no doubt the marriage is real." Grandfather looked at his wife. "Is there anything you'd like to add?"

Grandmother calmly set her teacup down in its saucer. "Yes, I think I would. I've seen the two of them together, and anyone with eyes can see that they care deeply for each other. That sort of love can't be faked. I won't let you ruin his life the way I stood by and let your father do to your brother and saw how it destroyed him. The best thing that ever happened to him was that woman. It stops here now. Landon is the heir to the title and the income that comes with it. If I hear one word that you've done anything to jeopardize it, I won't hesitate to instruct your father to take steps. Do I make myself clear?"

Landon was shocked at the steel he heard in the old woman's voice. Clearly, so was his uncle. "Yes, Mother."

She picked her cup up again. "Now that's all arranged, I think we should call the solicitor and get it signed off." Grandmother smiled serenely at her husband. "Don't you, dear?"

THEY'D DONE IT. Then why did Chora feel like crying instead of celebrating? Everyone was convinced they were the real deal. She still wasn't sure how they'd pulled it off, but they had. The looks Christina and Landon's uncle had sent their way had been so filthy to border on the ridiculous when it had become clear that the grandparents were going to side with Landon. And Landon... Her heart had swelled with happiness to hear his grandmother touch on what had happened between his parents and put their support behind him.

After that, it had been two short days. Two short days to continue the charade. Two short days in the country estate where they'd held hands and stared lovingly into each other's eyes. Two short days to hear more stories of growing up as a lord on a country estate. Two short days to hear about the wondrous Minoans and the secrets he still hoped to unravel. Two short days to fill a lifetime of memories of Landon.

Now that she sat in his car parked on the tarmac, his

plane waiting in front of them, everything about her felt frozen. When she'd called her charity to let them know that she would finally be coming home, it had seemed a relief, the thought of cuddling with her animals at night or hearing Mac-attack's new swear words something she'd looked forward to. Instead, her heart felt like it was being torn in two, like no matter where she was, a piece of it would always be missing.

Tormented, she looked at Landon. If only he didn't look so dang composed. If he could just throw her a crumb that he felt even the slightest in the way she did, she knew she would collapse at his feet and beg for them to try to make their marriage one for real. But how did one expose such vulnerability in the face of the British stiff upper lip?

"We'll, of course, continue to spend time together periodically when required." Landon stared out the windscreen at the gray London sky. *At least the weather got the memo.* "But I will make excuses that you are required by your charity, since obviously it has been neglected in the first flush of our marriage."

"Seems sensible."

"Luckily, most people won't keep track of who comes and goes to see me in Crete, and I can always claim we have spent more time together than we have."

"Luckily."

He shot her a sideways glance as if trying to gauge if she was being sarcastic or not. "By the end of the year, we will quietly divorce, and each be on our merry little way."

"Awesome."

"Obviously, I will hold up my end of the bargain and make sure you receive an allowance each year and also a lump sum when we divorce." He sat watching her expectantly.

Stunned, she realized that it really was all over. This

magical adventure they'd shared together had come to an end. Swallowing hard against the lump in her throat, she fumbled with the door as she opened it. Blinking rapidly, she knew he'd come around to her side before she could even see him. "I guess this is goodbye."

"Chora?"

Her heart leapt. "Yes?"

"Do you think maybe we should have one last kiss to say farewell? It seems somehow fitting."

Chora didn't know if she could possibly bear it but found herself powerless to resist nodding. Landon gathered her up in his arms like she was made of precious porcelain and she melted into his embrace as if she could meld them into one being. Divine ecstasy swirled through her when Landon's lips finally claimed her own. *Mine!* her heart screamed, fighting against the bittersweetness of the moment, defying her to tell Landon she loved him. All too soon, he pulled back, his burning gaze holding her breathlessly still as he reached out and gently stroked her cheek.

"I don't think I'll ever be able to step into the King's Chambers and not think of you. Goodbye, Chora." Before she could answer him, he turned and was gone.

Call him back. Tell him, demanded her heart. But coward that she was, she instead blindly found her way to the plane through her unshed tears. It was time to go home. *Alone.*

*P*eace, solitude, the whispers of the ancients. It was all Landon had ever needed to feel complete. Instead, now they taunted him at every turn, leaving him feeling empty and adrift. Since his return, he hadn't even been able to bring himself to venture near the Knossos Palace, let alone the King's Chambers, finding every possible excuse to give his colleagues. But in his heart, he couldn't hide the truth from himself. It was worse when he was sitting on the terrace. Time and again he found himself seeking Velchanos before remembering the hound would never feel the warmth of the sun on his hide again. The melancholy would take hold, and he found himself wishing for Chora to step out from the kitchen, a warm smile on her lips to drive the shadows away.

Today was the same as every day had been since Chora had left. Stepping in the front door, he was grateful that the housecleaner had been today and left the lights on. Somehow coming home to a dark house made it seem sadder. Maybe he should call his mother, but he already suspected he knew what she would say. She seemed to feel that one piece of advice fit most situations. *Follow your heart. Don't be like your father's family, you're better than that.* So far, she'd trotted the same piece of advice out when he'd wanted a pet giraffe, to move to Crete, and whether or not to become a Buddhist.

Spying the mail that had been left on the kitchen counter, he was surprised to see his grandmother's elegant script on a thick envelope. He wasn't sure when he'd last received a letter from either of his grandparents—they both much preferred to have their secretary do it for them. Come to think about it, even his notes from the tooth fairy had been typed.

Landon turned the off-white package over in his hand, running a hand over the dark blue ink. *Surely, if it was something bad, it would have come from Grandfather's desk.* Deciding it was to be treated much like a Band-Aid, he reached into the kitchen drawer and, using a paring knife, ripped it open.

Withdrawing the contents, he stared down at two distinct letters. One was yellowed with age, the script blockier, somehow more forceful, and the other one crisp white paper complete with his grandmother's letterhead. It seemed as good a place as any to begin.

Dear Landon,

As is often the case, as one gets older, one has the benefit of perspective. I would prefer that you know that I never did anything with malicious intent, however, things were done differently back when you father and mother were courting.

Your grandfather was right. Your mother was completely wrong to fit in with our family. She was, however, perfect for your father, and he should never have been forced to choose between love (which I think was something he'd never considered before) and the duty he was raised to hold above everything else. The worst thing a mother can ever realize is that the choice she forced on her child is the one that destroyed any hope they had of being happy.

When your father died, I found this letter amongst his belong-

ings. Maybe it wasn't about your mother fitting in with us, but us learning to be more like her. Seeing you with Chora, I feel like I have been granted a second chance at making things right.

Your loving Grandmother.

Stunned, Landon sat down heavily on a stool. The page contained words that she would never have expressed face to face, and yet it didn't make any of it less poignant. Swallowing, he tried to mentally prepare for what his father had to say from beyond the grave.

My Dearest Heart,

For one brief moment in my life, I was lucky enough to feel like the stars shone only for you and me. It is something that I have cherished through the dark years since. I was blinkered by what was indoctrinated into me from my birth, but that is no excuse. I should have believed in us. What fool chooses duty over love, especially the kind of love that we shared?

It is now as I lay here, feeling the coldness creep into my bones, that I finally have the strength to beg for your forgiveness. The day I drove you away, I ceased to live. I stagger under the guilt at the kind of father I have been to our son. The only hope are the flashes of you I see in him. I ask only that you never allow him to make the same mistake I did.

My hand is beginning to weaken. I find that I get tired easily now. Know that I will wait for you when your time comes—God willing, not too quickly—and I pray that you will once again allow me to hold you close.

Your always loving

Philip

Lightheaded, Landon numbly folded the paper. Somehow he felt like he was intruding on a private moment between his father and mother. *Did she even know this letter existed?* That was a matter for another time. He needed to get to the airport. There was somewhere he needed to be, or with someone. *Chora.*

MYSTERIOUSLY, the woman smiled, the snakes draped around as comfortably as if they were a part of her own body. Chora touched the glass between her and the urn, as close as she would get to Crete ever again. *I have more than I've ever wanted. Why do I feel so poor?* Landon had been true to his word. The house had been signed over to her, and more money than she knew how to spend appeared in her account each month.

The glumness never seemed to completely disappear, a perpetual fog that dampened any sense of happiness. It was here at the museum looking at fragments that belonged to that glorious time spent in Crete with Landon that she felt any real sense of peace.

"Aww, snakes," a young boy of no more than ten said beside her. Chora had been so engrossed in the sculpture that she hadn't noticed him before.

"Snakes aren't that bad," she said with a smile. "I actually like them more than some people I know."

"But why has she got them all over her like that?"

"Because in the Minoan civilization, snakes represented the reborn dead and feature in quite a few of their cults."

Chora's heart leapt into her mouth at the smooth cultured voice. *Landon!* Surely she was mistaken. Afraid to get her hopes up, she slowly turned, keeping her gaze on her feet until the last possible moment. "Are you really here?" Breathless, she could only stare, as if he'd disappear like a zephyr.

"Yes, I'm really here."

She desperately wanted to reach out and touch him. Suddenly, she felt shy, as if, no matter that he was standing there right in front of her, somehow, he might as well still be in Crete. "How did you know I was here?"

"Your housekeeper told me. Well, after I finished helping her chase some rabbits. By the way, when did Mac-attack start learning to swear in Greek?" The idea seemed to delight him.

"Oh, well, um, it was just something I started when I got back." It had been cathartic on the lonely evenings. "Has something happened? Did your grandparents change their minds?" Chora blurted out, the suspense too much for her.

"No." He quickly moved closer, taking hold of her hands. "Everything's fine."

"Then why are you here?"

"Because something occurred to me. A mystery that I never thought I'd unravel. Suddenly the answer was right in front of me."

"You deciphered Linear A? Oh my goodness, I'm so happy for you."

He blinked at her, a fond smile curving his lips. "No, and I'm not saying that wouldn't be amazing, because it would be, but I think this is even better." Chora frowned at him. *What could possibly be better than that?* "I discovered this wonderfully brilliant woman I managed to convince to marry me"— Landon wagged a finger at her—"in name only. Well, somehow, and I'm not sure how because it rather snuck up on me, I'm madly in love with her."

Chora swallowed the lump in her throat. It wouldn't have surprised her if it had been her heart leaping right out of her chest. "You are?"

Landon tenderly stared into her eyes. "I am."

She blinked tears away. "That wasn't the plan."

"I know."

"I didn't stick with the plan either."

"Are you saying what I think you're saying?"

"I love you, too."

Landon's lips grazed hers, a whisper soft kiss sending a

delicious shiver down her spine, before he pulled away. "This is where I'd normally ask you to marry me, but we've already done that. Instead, would you be my wife in heart and soul?"

How could she say no when he already had both? "They're yours, now and forever. Will you be my husband in heart and soul?"

He gently caressed her cheek with his hand, never once breaking the gaze between them. "Without you, I have no heart. You are my soul." As he pulled her back into him again, his mouth claiming hers, Chora knew she would never be lost again. Not with this man by her side.

"It's absolutely ghastly being around the pair of you. You know that, right?" Freddy drawled.

"It's bloody sickening," Alistair agreed, sticking his tongue out at the disgustingly in love pair across the table from him.

"At least they had the good manners to be married before they decided to fall in love. Jolly good show," Stirling congratulated them.

"Thank you," Chora giggled. "You know, it would do all of you the world of good to fall in love."

"I thought we were friends." Freddy looked mortally wounded.

"We are, and that's why we want you to be as happy as we are." Chora smiled adoringly at her husband. "Isn't that right?"

"Of course, dear," Landon agreed, gazing tenderly back at her.

"So, it's the royal 'we' now, is it?" Alistair said. "And that's a definite no from me, too."

"Can you imagine any of us married?" Stirling asked. "Why would you wish that on a poor girl?"

"Maybe the right girl for you isn't a girl, but a woman who knows how to handle you." Chora gave him a saucy wink.

"Is that how you caught the fine fellow sitting beside you?" Freddy returned her wink as he reached for his drink.

"I like to think I gave her an offer she couldn't refuse," Landon answered indulgently.

"On that topic, when are we to expect offspring from the two of you? I'm sure your grandparents have already made their wishes clear." Alistair swept the room with his gaze, always on the lookout for the next willing companion.

"You know they have." Landon chuckled heartily. "But we've been granted a reprieve for a few years."

"It helps that they know kids are something we definitely want, just not right now," Chora hastily added. "Right now, we want to enjoy this time together, just the two of us, living each day as an adventure."

The friends looked at each other. As she spoke, it was as if she had somehow lost focus on them, only Landon filling her senses. Shuddering as one, all three men took a drink. *No, thank you.*

THE END

As an Indie Author, reviews help me get my books noticed. If you enjoyed reading Landon and Chora's story as much as I did writing it, please leave a review. It will make all the difference to me.

If you loved, *The Cowgirl's Fake Billionaire Marriage*, sign up for my newsletter here to get the free bonus's and exclusive news. Now, turn the page to discover my new series, *Billionaires Lonely Hearts Club* beginning with Alistair's story, *Red Dust and the Billionaire*

SNEAK PEEK NEW SERIES
BILLIONAIRES LONELY HEARTS
CLUB – RED DUST AND THE
BILLIONAIRE

Alistair might have spent most of his life surrounded by the green English countryside, but that didn't mean red dust didn't flow through his veins. When he'd been no taller than knee-high to a grasshopper, his grandfather had taken him everywhere with him and he'd return from his adventures bursting to tell his parents about all that he had seen and learned. From the ranges of Western Australia looking at iron ore deposits to the spinifex country of one of many cattle properties the family owned, he had always known that one day he would answer the call and return home.

He'd never expected the call would be for his grandfather's funeral. Somehow, he'd seemed indestructible. In fact, his nickname had been Tungsten for his unyielding manner and strength. But even the toughest is made weak in the face of old age. Grandfather had lived a remarkable life and now the mantle would fall to Father. Alistair rather pitied Dad. Those shoes would be impossible to fill.

Speak of the devil. His father sat down beside him. "Dad always wanted you to have a chance to have your freedom, sow your wild oats and all that, but now it's time for you to come home." His voice changed, vulnerability creeping in. "I'm going to need you here."

"Dad, whatever you need me to do, I'll do it." Family always came first, no matter what.

"I was hoping you'd say that. One of the operations in the Northern Territory needs some attention. There's a new station manager there now, but thanks to the old one, the profitability of the place has been ruined. If you can oversee it while the new one gets up to speed, it would be one less thing for me to worry about. Right now, I need to focus on our Iron Ore Holdings." There was a tight wariness to him, like he couldn't relax, fearful of what would happen if he did.

Alistair nodded, rapidly considering all that he would need to put into place back in England. "Give me a month and I'll be ready to take the reins."

His father clapped him heartily on the shoulder. "One month, son, and you'll finally be fully back in the family fold."

Alistair smiled back at him, determined that he would straighten out the mess for his dad, therefore taking away at least one weight from the burden he carried. After all, it was the least he could do in memory of his grandfather.

Red Dust and the Billionaire available on Amazon and in Kindle Unlimited here

ACKNOWLEDGMENTS

A debt of gratitude to my editor Rebekah Groves for her patience with me.

Another big thanks to Megan from Designed with Grace for her cover design.

To my amazing beta readers and street team, you guys rock and I couldn't do it without you.

And finally to my fabulous alpha reader Trixie Norman, for all the late nights of reading and endless questions about your thoughts.

Red Dust and The Billionaire

Alistair's Story Coming Soon...

Pre Order Now

Star Dust and The Billionaire

Stirling's Story Coming Soon...

Pre Order Now

Gold Dust and The Billionaire

Freddy's Story Coming Soon...

Pre Order Now

Cowboy Christmas Series

<u>The Mistletoe Collection</u>

Boots and Mistletoe

Cowboy boots, mistletoe, and a holiday do-over...

Buy Now

The Cowboy Under the Mistletoe

It'll take more than the magic of the season to help this grump find her happily ever after...

Buy Now

Mistletoe and the Billionaire's Cowgirl

He's the last man she wants this holiday season. Too bad he's exactly what she needs...

Buy Now

Barrels and Hearts series

Available on Amazon and Kindle Unlimited

A Bull Rider's Paradise

The prequel to the Barrels and Hearts series. True love is only the beginning….of the story. Find out where it all began with Ana and Eduardo. Sometimes finding love is easy. It's keeping it that's hard.

Buy here

A Cowgirl's Dream

An Aussie cowgirl far from home. A handsome Brazilian bull rider. Can they have a rodeo love story of their dreams?

Buy Now

A Cowgirl's Heart

An Aussie cowgirl in need. Her childhood friend to the rescue. Can friendship turn into a love story?

Buy Now

A Cowgirl's Passion

One feisty cowgirl. One steadfast Brazilian bull rider. Will she see what is right in front of her?

Buy Now

A Cowgirl's Pride

An Aussie cowgirl from the wrong side of the tracks. A handsome equine vet. Can they find a way to have their happy ever after?

Buy Now

A Cowgirl's Love

A young Aussie cowgirl. A widowed rancher. Does age matter when it comes to love?

Buy Now

A Cowgirl's Movie Star

A fiery cowgirl with big dreams. A movie star far from home. When their two worlds collide, will their love be strong enough to hold them together or will they be pulled apart

Buy Now

A Cowgirl's Billionaire

A cowgirl adrift. A broken billionaire cowboy. Can he free himself from the past to be the man she needs now?

Buy Now

ABOUT THE AUTHOR

Edith MacKenzie or Eddie Mac to her friends is an author of sweet and wholesome contemporary cowboy romance. They say in literary circles to write what you know, and Eddie has certainly taken that to heart. Before embarking on a writing career, she trained horses professionally and brings that wealth of knowledge to her writing.

Now a mum to a boy and girl, as well as wife, she delights with her tales of strong cowgirls and their adventures in finding love. When not weaving the love stories of her characters, she enjoys hanging out with her family and animals, as well as reading, fishing and camping.

Just remember—once a cowgirl, always a cowgirl.

facebook.com/EddieMacAuthor
instagram.com/edith_mackenzie_author
amazon.com/Edith-MacKenzie
bookbub.com/profile/edith-mackenzie
twitter.com/edith_mackenzie